FLY PAPER

Books *by* Max Allan Collins

Nolan Novels

FLY PAPER

HARD CASH

SCRATCH FEVER

HUSH MONEY

MOURN THE LIVING

SPREE

Quarry Novels

QUARRY

QUARRY'S LIST

QUARRY'S DEAL

QUARRY'S CUT

QUARRY'S VOTE

from PERFECT CRIME BOOKS

FLY PAPER

MAX ALLAN COLLINS

With an Introduction by the Author

PERFECT CRIME BOOKS

Printed in the United States of America.

Perfect Crime Books™ is a registered Trademark.

Cover by Christopher Mills.

Library of Congress Cataloging-in-Publication Data
Collins, Max Allan
Fly Paper/Max Allan Collins

ISBN: 978-1-935797-22-7

Perfect Crime Books Edition: May 2012

This is for Terry Beatty,
who understands Jon.

"*Sky piracy . . . involves the interests of every nation, the safety of every traveller, and the integrity of that structure of order on which a world community depends.*"

R. M. Nixon

"*Take me to Mexico.*"

D. B. Cooper

Introduction

WHILE IT WAS NICE to have Hard Case Crime bring the first two Nolan novels–*Bait Money* and *Blood Money*–back into print in a single volume (*Two for the Money*), that republication proved something of a dead-end. Charles Ardai, the visionary editor at Hard Case, was particularly keen to republish *Blood Money*, his favorite of the Nolan novels, and he only merged it with *Bait Money* at my request. Charles has also made clear he's open to a new Nolan novel, but expressed no interest in bringing out the other existing entries in the series.

That series, like most of my series, began with what was intended to be a one-shot novel, *Bait Money*, written in the late sixties and early seventies when I was at the Writers Workshop at the University of Iowa in Iowa City. I had grown up wanting to write "tough guy" fiction, very much in the thrall of Spillane, Hammett, Chandler, Cain and Thompson, but had recently discovered the Richard Stark-bylined "Parker" novels by Donald E. Westlake. Don became something of a mentor to me, and he said nice things about *Bait Money*, even though it was obviously in part an homage to his own series about a hardbitten professional thief.

That book originally had Nolan dying at the conclusion–my thinking being that once is homage, twice is rip-off–but when the publisher, Curtis Books, asked for sequels, I said yes. (Don was kind enough to give his blessing, saying that the Jon character, Nolan's youthful sidekick, humanized both Nolan and the series itself in a way that was quite apart from his Stark novels.)

Blood Money was an outgrowth of dangling plot threads from *Bait Money*. Since Nolan had originally kicked the bucket in that book, at the hands of a former Family boss of his (the Family being my name for the Mob or the Outfit), plenty of loose ends awaited tying off.

So in a way, *Fly Paper* was the first true series entry. It was tricky because Nolan had retired from professional crime and was trying to go straight, in his jagged way. That meant to some degree all of the novels have, like *Blood Money*, grown from the previous ones. The series, in a way, is one long sprawling novel that resolves in *Spree*, and perhaps that's why I've never written another.

The idea of the crook trying to go straight, and having his past come back at him in a bad karmic fashion, is the heart of these novels. Nolan is not a guy who has gotten religion, not hardly–he has always been a capitalist, a businessman chasing the American dream, and nothing grandiose, either.

Fly Paper grew out of the basic idea of, "What if a tough

guy of Nolan's stripe had been on board when D. B. Cooper famously skyjacked a plane?" This also provided an opportunity to make the D. B. Cooper character sympathetic, and pursue what has been a recurring plot device in my work: sending two sympathetic, opposing forces up against each other, to fuck with the reader.

It also gave me the opportunity to create a new recurring source of opposition for Nolan, now that his score with the Chicago Family was more or less settled. The Comfort family (lower case "f") became that new collective adversary for Nolan, and they are among my proudest creations, part Scraggs from *Li'l Abner*, with a dose of various characters Strother Martin played in '60s and '70s movies, and a big dollop of a real rural family of miscreants who used to love to come hear my band Crusin' play, back (as they say) in the day.

Fly Paper was written around 1973, and was unfortunate enough to go into publishing limbo, when Curtis Books was bought up by Popular Library, who (despite assurances) never got around to publishing the four Nolan novels in their inventory. I didn't get the rights back until the early '80s, when all of the books (*Bait Money* through *Scratch Fever*) were purchased by Pinnacle Books. In the intervening almost-a-decade, security measures at airports had heightened and that required a minor rewrite. Now those updated security measures seem mild indeed.

My thanks to the readers who've asked to see these books, as well as to John Boland at Perfect Crime Books for giving Nolan another shot at the American dream.

MAX ALLAN COLLINS
January 2012

Prologue: Pre-Flight Check

THE SUITCASE ITSELF was a bomb. It would be harmless enough going through baggage check, and no matter how roughly it was tossed into the cargo hold, it wouldn't explode: all the jostle in the world couldn't do that. *Not till I arm it,* he thought. By remote control, when the plane is in the air. Even then, nothing could set it off. Except his finger, on the right button.

Not that he *wanted* to blow up a plane, killing all the people on board, himself included. He wanted no part of that. But it was a possibility, a calculated risk he had to take; high stakes, high risk, simple as that. A more desperate man wouldn't have twitched an eye at such a prospect, and his concern for his own life and the lives of others was proof positive that he was anything but a desperate man.

He was, rather, a man who'd made a decision. A difficult one at that, reached through calm, rational consideration. And as for the plane blowing up and people getting killed, well, that would be someone else's decision: the decision of the airline official or FBI agent or heroic crew member who might force upon him the pushing of that final button.

He'd decided, too, that only under the most extreme circumstances would he even consider pushing that button before all the passengers (except a handful of hostages) were off the plane. He was not a monster, after all: the killing of perhaps several hundred people was not something his conscience could easily bear, even if that killing was forced upon him. Of course if it came to that, his conscience would be blown to pieces along with everything and everybody else, wouldn't it?

But that was the most far-fetched of possibilities. That was not according to his plan. This is how it will go, he thought: after commandeering the plane, he would direct the pilot to a specific airport, at which the bulk of the passengers would be allowed to disembark. Remaining on the plane would be crew members (pilot, copilot and navigator), as well as a stewardess (a volunteer) and some passenger hostages (likewise volunteers). After the ransom money was delivered, the passenger hostages would be released, and the plane would again take off.

He felt no moral responsibility toward the lives of any of these people. The crew members were, after all, professionals highly paid to bear the hazards of flying, including that of skyjacking. And likewise, he couldn't be expected to feel concerned about the passengers who volunteered to stay on as hostages. They would be volunteers, who'd made their own decision to stay on the plane, wouldn't they? He was not responsible.

He was twenty-six years old and looked eighteen, with an eternally boyish face, like Johnny Carson. His hair was fair and short, neatly trimmed, neatly combed; he was freckled and blue-eyed. Despite the sloppiness of his surroundings, he was dressed in conservative, tidy work clothes: a deep brown sweatshirt with the words "Greystoke Teacher's College" spelled out in white, light brown jeans, brown Hush Puppies and dark socks. His was the type of appearance many fathers long for in their sons; he was just what the recruiting officer was looking for: he was clean-cut.

He was hunched over the workbench in a basement that looked like a warehouse of a small electronics firm after a rather untidy burglary. While the workbench itself was well ordered, the room surrounding was chaos: supplies, abandoned projects, empty cartons, stacks of Radio Shack and other electronics catalogs, all were scattered about like so much refuse. Still, mess or no mess, he knew where to find whatever he needed, whenever he needed. To the uninitiated, the basement was a mess; to him it was a filing system.

The basement also held the artifacts of a childhood not entirely given up: a table with an electric train, still functioning, though one would have had to do a ballet around the boxes and unfinished projects to get to the control; a go-cart, mostly disassembled, awaiting the mood to strike its owner to put Humpty Dumpty back together; a guitar amplifier he'd half finished back in early high school, when he'd thought for a while he might take up that instrument; a motorcycle from that same era, a lightweight Honda, also still functioning, or almost—as soon as he got the engine put back together it would be; and off in one corner, stacks of science fiction comic books and pulp digests, as well as an overflowing box of tattered Big Little Books, space stuff mostly ("Buck Rogers," "Flash Gordon," "Brick Bradford"), old junk left from his older brother's childhood but also a fond part of his. The yellowed pages of those little books, as well as the s-f comics and pulps he'd bought himself, stirred his sense of adventure as much in their way as the go-cart and Honda had in theirs.

Upstairs, his wife kept things orderly. When they'd moved to this modest but cozy house from their small apartment (which had been more his workshop than their apartment, every room but the bath looking not unlike this basement), she had asked him if he could limit his projects and such to the downstairs. Though he could have overriden her if he'd wanted to, he'd deferred to her wishes. After all, she was his wife and deserved a nice home, didn't she? He stayed downstairs.

Now he was rechecking all his leads, making doubly sure they were firmly soldered to the various solid-state chips that made up his remote control system. He was good at this sort of thing. He was an all-around handyman, good at anything mechanical—no electronics genius, maybe, but he knew what he was doing. There were guys with degrees in chemistry and biophysics and the like (his degree was in business) who had the knowledge, sure, but not the knack, not the knack for putting things together, making them work. He could make something out of nothing. Give him a pile of junk and a little time, and he would provide the sweat and imagination and come up with something special. The suitcase/bomb, for instance. He'd made that from, well, he'd made it from crap. Literally. Fertilizer, that is, nitrate-based fertilizer purchased at a local farm supply outlet. The nitrates were the key, and utilizing a variation on standard industrial "cook-book" recipes, he'd had no trouble processing the nitrate-based fertilizer into 10 x 4 x 3-inch blocks of plastic explosive, which looked like nothing more than six loaves of unbaked rye bread.

Next to the suitcase on the work bench were three items of great importance.

The first was a light, compact, but serviceable parachute, one he'd used when skydiving was a hobby of his several years ago, an emergency chute, worn strapped to the stomach.

Next was a portable citizen's band radio, sender/receiver, about the size of a small hardcover book; this would provide communications when he hit the ground, so that his wife could come pick him up (she'd be receiving and sending on a C.B. in the car). The C.B. had a black, slightly padded case with a clip that would slip over his belt.

And, finally, there was the pocket calculator, an inconspicuous block of black plastic with numbered push-button face, not much bigger or thicker than a deck of playing cards. In this case, however, the deck was decidedly stacked: he had wired in several special functions in addition to the calculator's usual ones. Except for a chip of circuitry that ran the calculator (whose bulk was primarily due to the panel of push buttons, and the window that displayed the answer to whatever mathematical question you might ask via those buttons) the inside was hollow, and there'd been plenty of space for the extra wiring. He'd wired in a signal, using a frequency higher than the regular broadcast band, one that would penetrate sufficiently into the cargo hold of the plane. This high frequency would be diffracted throughout the entire compartment, seeking out the suitcase, whereas a lower frequency would be blocked out by the metal of the plane.

Four times four would arm the suitcase/bomb. Four times four times four would detonate.

"Honey!"

His wife. Carol. He covered the suitcase with some newspapers and went upstairs to her, before she could come down.

She was in the kitchen, sitting at the yellow formica top table, stirring cream and sugar into a cup of coffee. She'd been crying again. Crying made most girls less attractive; ran their mascara and everything. His wife was different. Crying didn't spoil her looks at all: she was a natural beauty, wore practically no makeup, just a touch of pale pink lip gloss. She had long, cascading blonde hair. Natural. Her eyes were cornflower blue. While her nose was a trifle large, it was nicely formed, and she had a nice white smile, too, though she wasn't showing it now. Only on the occasional times when he stopped and studied her like this did he realize how really beautiful she was, and how good it was to have her around.

Like her hair, the kitchen was yellow, except for the white appliances that Carol kept so highly polished that when morning sun came in the window and reflected off them, it was almost blinding. Right now, however, the kitchen was dark, gloomy dark. It was the middle of the evening, and the window next to the table, curtain drawn back, let in nothing but moonless night. She'd left windows open all around the house, and though it was late October, the breeze was just cool, nothing more. No sounds came from outside: the night sounds in Canker, Missouri, population 12,000, ran to little more than the sporadic squealing of a teenager's tires. What little light there was in the kitchen came from the living room where the TV was going, unattended; a comedy show was on, volume low, but every now and then a rumble of canned laughter would break the stillness. Carol's face was pale. Expressionless.

"What's wrong, Carol?"

"I don't want you to do it."

"Carol."

"Ken. Honey. I don't want you to go through with it."

"And I don't want to discuss that anymore. I already made up my mind. This is one project I'm going to finish."

"Sit down, will you? And talk to me?"

He sat down, but he didn't say anything.

"What are you working on downstairs?"

"You know. What I told you."

"Why's it taking so long to put together? I mean, if it's a fake bomb, why's it taking so long?"

"I explained that. It has to look realistic. It'll help me if they have to waste a lot of hours defusing what they think is a bomb." That didn't really make much sense, but fortunately, she hadn't questioned the logic of it.

"Ken?"

"Yes?"

"I don't understand you."

"Sure you do."

"I don't. I don't understand any of this. It seems so unnecessary . . ."

"Carol. Look at my face. It's got lines in it. I'm a kid and I got lines in my face." It was something that was bothering him lately. Not that he was vain, but he did like to think of himself as young, and damn it, he was young. But his features, while boyish as ever and always would be, had grown tight these few years past; crow's feet at the eyes, deep lines in his face from frowning too much and from smiling too much, too. He'd been a salesman these last three years, and excessive frowning (to himself, in private)

7

and smiling (at prospective buyers, in public) were inescapable hazards of the trade. It came, as they said, with the territory.

"Still, honey," Carol was saying, "you're not old. Really. Would it be so hard to start over?"

"It sure would. You want me to die of a heart attack by thirty? I mean, look at my face, the lines. Jeez."

Tears were welling up in her eyes. Even in the dark he could see that. Out in the living room, the TV was laughing.

"Come on, Carol. Knock it off. It's going to work out okay."

"Ken?"

"What?"

"You wouldn't hurt anybody, would you, honey?"

"You know me better than that, don't you? Jeez, Carol. How can you even say that."

She touched his hand, stroked it. "You want some coffee?"

"Okay. Then I got to get back downstairs and finish up."

One

1

SOMEBODY WAS BANGING at the side door. Jon ignored it for a while, focusing his attention on the late movie he was watching—the original 1933 *King Kong*. But the banging was insistent and finally, reluctantly, Jon pulled away from the TV and headed downstairs to see what inconsiderate S.O.B. had the crazy idea something was important enough to go around bothering people in the middle of *King Kong*. *Better be pretty damn earth-shaking,* Jon thought, *pisses me off,* and yanked open the door and saw a heavy-set man leaning against the side of the building, his shirt and hands covered with blood. The guy had blood on his face, too, and looked at Jon and rasped, "Who . . . who the hell are you?"

Which took the words right out of Jon's mouth.

Up until then, it had been a normal day. He'd risen around noon, showered, got dressed, thrown some juice down, and gone out front to the box to see if he'd gotten any comic books in the mail. Jon was a comics freak, a dedicated collector of comic art in all its forms, and did a lot of mail-order buying and trading with other buffs around the country.

He was also an aspiring comics artist himself (as yet unpublished), and while he was disappointed to find no letters of acceptance for any of the artwork he'd sent off, so too was he relieved to find no rejections.

Jon was twenty-one years old, a short but powerfully built kid (he was such a comics nut that he'd actually sent in for that Charles Atlas course advertised on the back of the books) with a full head of curly brown hair and intense blue eyes. He also had a turned-up nose that he despised and that girls, thankfully, found cute. His dress ran to worn jeans, and T-shirts picturing various comic strip heroes, everything from Wonder Warthog of the underground comics to Captain Marvel (Shazam!) of the forties "Golden Age" of comics. Today he had a Flash Gordon short-sleeve sweatshirt; the artwork (a full-figure shot of Flash with cape) was by Alex Raymond, the late creator of Flash. Jon would accept no substitutes.

You see, comics were Jon's life.

Take his room, for example. When his uncle had first given it to him, this room was a dreary storeroom in the back of the antique shop, a cement-floored, gray-wood-walled cubicle about as cheerful as a Death Row cell. Now it was a bright reflection of Jon's love for comic art. The walls were literally papered with colorful posters depicting such heroes as Dick Tracy, Batman, Buck Rogers, and the aforementioned Flash Gordon, all drawn by Jon himself in pen and ink and watercolored, and were uncanny recreations of the characters, drawn in their original style. (That was both a skill and a problem of Jon's: while his eye for copying technique was first-rate, he had no real style of his own. "Give me time," Jon would say to the invisible critics, "give me time.") Shag throw rugs covered the floors in splashes of cartoon color, and the walls were lined three deep with the boxes containing his voluminous collection of plastic-bagged and filed comic books, a file cabinet in one corner the keeper of the more precious of his pop artifacts. A drawing easel with swivel chair was against the wall, a brimming wastebasket next to it, and sheets of drawing paper and Zip-a-Tone backing lay at the easel's feet like oversize dandruff. And the two pieces of antique walnut furniture his uncle had given him were not exempt from comics influence, either: the chest of drawers had bright underground comics decals stuck all over its rich wood surface (Zippy, the Freak Brothers, Mr. Natural), and on top Jon's pencils, pens, brushes, and bottles of ink were scattered among the cans of deodorant and shave cream and other necessities. Even the finely carved headboard of his bed was spotted with taped-on scraps of Jon's artwork, cartoonish sketches of this and that, mostly character studies of his girl, Karen, and Nolan, and his Uncle Planner.

His Uncle Planner. Still hard to think of Planner as being dead. Just a few months since it happened, and though Jon was almost used to the absence of the old man, he still didn't like living alone in the big, dusty old antique shop. Soon he'd be getting around to contacting some people to come in and appraise and bid on the merchandise in the store. Planner's collection of antique political buttons alone would bring a pretty penny. Of course the stuff in the front of the store, the long, narrow "showroom" of supposed antiques, was junk, crap Planner had picked up at yard sales and flea markets just to keep the shop sufficiently stocked; the good stuff was in the back rooms, because when Planner had run across actual antiques, he'd crated them up carefully and packed them away. Jon's uncle had had real respect for real antiques, and felt it was silly to sell them, as their value was sure to increase day by day. Jon, however, had no hesitation about selling those back-room treasures, though he'd do his best to find a buyer who'd haul away the junk as well as the jewels.

Mostly, of course, the shop had been a front for Jon's uncle. Planner had been just what his name implied: he planned things—specifically, jobs for professional thieves. He'd traveled around on "buying trips" and, in the role of cantankerous old antique dealer, had gathered the information necessary to put together successful "packages" for professional heist men like Nolan. Planner's packages were detailed and precise, at times even including blueprints of the target, and he'd charged a fee plus percentage of the take. Two years ago, with the guidance of his uncle, Jon had participated in the execution of one of those packages, a bank robbery headed by Nolan (whom Planner rated as perhaps the best in a dying craft), and some three quarters of a million dollars from that robbery had rested in Planner's safe since then—until this summer, when two men with guns came into the antique shop and shot Planner dead and took the money.

Jon and Nolan had gone after the two men and the money, and caught the two men, all right, but the money was lost. And so was Jon's dream of owning a comic book shop, a mecca for collectors like himself—as were his hopes for having enough money to support himself for as long as it took to break into the comic art field. All of that—up in smoke.

But not really. As Planner's sole heir, he was now owner of the shop, which he could conceivably convert into his comic book mecca, even if its location (Iowa City, Iowa) was a bit off the beaten track. And he had those two back rooms full of valuable antiques to turn into cash. And, too, Nolan had told him that the next time something came together, Jon was the first man he'd call. So things weren't so awfully bleak, really.

Jon returned to his room with the mail (not much—just some bills and the latest issue of *The Buyer's Guide for Comics Fandom*) and flopped on the bed, his eye catching the poster of Lee Van Cleef on the wall over his easel. The Van Cleef poster was one of a few posters in the room that were photographic and not his own drawings. Van Cleef was in his "man-in-black" gunfighter stance and, it seemed to Jon, resembled Nolan a great deal: they shared the same narrow eyes, mustache, high cheekbones and genuinely hard, hawkish look, though Nolan could get an even surlier look going, if that was possible.

He wondered for a moment if Nolan was just being nice when he'd promised to contact Jon when something came up.

No.

Jon was sure Nolan had been telling the truth. He knew that Nolan felt responsible for the loss of their money, and that sooner or later Nolan would come to Jon with a plan to get them both back on their financial feet again.

Karen had once suggested to Jon that he was using Nolan as a father substitute, a bullshit idea that embarrassed and irritated Jon; why, he wouldn't even talk about it, it was such dime-store bullshit psychology. He'd never needed his real parents; why the fuck should he need a fake one? His father was just some guy his mother knew before Jon was born; and his mother was just a fourth-rate saloon singer who was on the road all the time, leaving him to shuttle back and forth between one relative or another, none of them particularly grateful for an extra mouth to feed. A few years ago, his mother had died in an automobile mishap, and he hadn't even shed a tear; he simply hadn't known her that well. Early on he'd developed a capacity for amusing himself, for losing himself in the four-color fantasy of the funnies, for being a self-sufficient loner. And, in fact, when he moved to Iowa City to attend the university (briefly, as it turned out), he'd taken a cubbyhole apartment for himself rather than move in with a relative again, even if that relative was Planner, the most pleasant of the lot. Only after the robbery last year, when Nolan had stayed at Planner's, healing from gunshot wounds, only then had Jon moved in with his uncle. And that was to help his uncle help Nolan.

His life since meeting Nolan had been hectic but exciting, tragic but exhilarating. Nolan's reality put the fantasy of Jon's comic book super-heroes to shame. Reality was harsh—in fantasy, Planner would still be alive, and last year's bank job wouldn't have erupted into insanity and blood—but, as Nolan might have said, jerking off is less trouble than screwing but it's nowhere near as rewarding.

The Van Cleef poster seemed to be squinting skeptically over at Flash Gordon, as if knowing how ridiculous it was of Jon to equate Nolan with comic book heroes. Ridiculous to think of Nolan as any kind of hero. But Jon did. Even though Nolan was a thief. The way Jon saw it, heroism had nothing to do with morality, or just causes, or politics, or anything else. Heroism had to do with courage; derring- do;

a personal code; a steel eye and cool head. And all of these Nolan had. Plenty of.

Jon thumbed through *The Buyer's Guide* (a weekly newspaper of comics-related ads and articles) and saw some photos of a comics convention held out on the West Coast. He wished for a moment he'd gone to Detroit for the convention there this coming weekend; today was Thursday and the start of the con. He'd attended the New York Comic Con several years running, but hadn't been to too many of the countless other such fandom gatherings. Seemed a pity with a con located here in the Midwest, for a change, that he hadn't been able to go.

But this weekend was Karen's birthday, and he had to be here. She would be justifiably hurt if he chose comics over her. And this would be a traumatic birthday for her: Karen would be turning thirty-one, and the ten-year difference in their ages would be shoved to the front of her awareness. It was something that didn't bother Jon in the least, but Karen was somewhat paranoid about it. The only thing Jon didn't like about Karen being older than he was (and divorced) was her ten-year-old freckle-faced brat, Larry, a red-headed refugee from a Keane painting, who was the best argument for birth control Jon could think of.

Which was something he was very much conscious of when, an hour-and-a-half later, he was having a late lunch with Karen at the Hamburg Inn; now that school was started again, he could enjoy her lunchtime company minus Larry. Bliss.

Jon and Karen had been semi-shacked-up for six months now. *Semi*-shacked because Jon hadn't really moved in with Karen (and vice versa) for the simple reason that Jon and Larry didn't get along, and besides, Karen thought it might be bad for Larry if Mommy's boy friend lived with them. A quaint idea in these loose days, Jon thought, but he didn't bitch: he liked his moments of privacy, and no way was he going to have his comic book collection and Larry under the same roof. It was a pleasant enough relationship as it was, and Karen was happy receiving the healthy alimony/child support check from her lawyer ex-husband (which would stop, of course, if she and Jon were to marry), and Jon had promised himself he wouldn't consider marriage with Karen until Larry was either old enough to send to military school or got hit by a truck.

Still, Jon *had* toyed with the idea of asking Karen to move in with him—even if Larry *did* have to come along. Karen ran the Candle Corner, a downtown Iowa City gift shop with head-shop overtones: hash pipes, Zig-Zag papers, posters, water beds, and the rack of underground comics that had brought Jon into Karen's shop in the first place. He'd considered asking her to help him convert Planner's antique shop into a larger version of her shop downtown, with more emphasis on water beds and apartment furnishings, and he would restrict his "comic book mecca" idea to a mail-order business out of one of the back rooms. She'd have no trouble interesting someone in taking over her long-term lease on that three-story building downtown that housed her shop, her apartment, and another to let above; and she and (ugh) Larry could move in with Jon, since the whole upstairs of the antique shop was a nicely remodeled five-room living quarters that Planner had used. So far, however, Jon had stayed in his room downstairs, only using the upstairs for its kitchen facilities and the living room's color TV, and that last only lately: it had taken Jon weeks to get used to the idea of Planner being dead and longer to lose the creepy feeling the upstairs gave him.

Anyway, he was considering that—asking Karen to move

in, to become his business partner. But he hesitated, and when he'd put in a long-distance call to Nolan (who had met Karen), to ask his opinion of the idea, the following advice had come from Nolan: "Never mix bed partners and business partners, kid—you get fucked both ways." And since Nolan tended to be right about such things, Jon was, for the present, holding off asking Karen.

He spent the afternoon drawing, working up rough pencil layouts for a science fiction story he was hoping to sell to *Heavy Metal* magazine. It was to be somewhat in the style of the old EC *Weird Fantasy* and *Weird Science*, two great but long-dead comics, casualties of the bloody war waged upon comic books by parental groups and psychiatrists back in the early fifties. Jon's script was two Ray Bradbury stories put together and all switched around, and for the art he was combining elements of the underground's Corben and EC's Wally Wood in hopes of disguising his own lack of style with a weird mixture.

At four o'clock he watched a "Star Trek" rerun.

At five he went across the street to the Dairy Queen for supper—a tenderloin and hot fudge sundae. He usually ate with Karen, but she was at a Tupperware party, for Christ's sake. ("You're going to a *Tupperware* party, Karen? What kind of free spirit are you, anyway? Hash pipes, water beds, and Tupperware!" "Jonny, she's a friend of mine. She's one of my best friends and she invited me; I have to go. If you're not busy . . . could you sit with Larry?" "Anything but that, Kare. Let me pay for the damn sitter myself. Anything.")

At six-thirty he got out a stack of comic books he hadn't gotten around to yet and started reading.

At ten he went upstairs and turned on the TV and got himself a bottle of Coke and some potato chips and got settled down for the showing of *King Kong* on the educational channel at ten-thirty.

At eleven-thirty somebody knocked on the back door.

The man with bloody hands and shirt.

2

THE NIGHT AFTER Sherry left, Nolan was consumed with boredom and hostility, and felt he had to get away from the motel for an evening or he'd go fucking crazy. The motel was called the Tropical, and Nolan had been managing the place for some syndicate people out of Chicago for months now, but it was a job he'd grown tired of lately, and he had to let off steam. Since he didn't care to embarrass or anger his employers, he took the time to drive some fifty miles to a little town where nobody knew him and, dressed in the grubbiest old clothes he could dig up, spent the evening in a tawdry little pool hall with the village's "rougher element," people who would have been born on the wrong side of the tracks had the town been big enough to have tracks.

Nolan was good at shooting pool. He was hustler-good, but chose to shoot by himself, and did so undisturbed for two solid hours, drinking beer and doing his best to run the balls as rapidly as possible. Tonight he was off a little, as his mind was busy with Sherry and the job at the Tropical and ways of changing what was becoming a tiresome life.

He was fifty years old, even if he didn't look it, a tall, raw-boned man with just a little gut from several months of overly easy, overly soft living. His hair was black, widow's-peaked, with considerable gray working its way in along his sideburns; he wore a down-curving mustache that made his mouth take on an even more sour expression than it naturally wore; he had high cheekbones, and his face had a chiseled look, like something turned out by a sculptor in a black mood.

He had been a professional thief for almost twenty years, an organizer and leader of robberies, mostly institutional (banks, jewelry stores, armored cars, and the like) and his was the best track record in the business: there was not and never had been a single member of a Nolan heist behind bars—though some were in jail for other, non-Nolan jobs they'd been in on, and a few did die in double-cross attempts Nolan squelched.

Before that, when he was just a kid, really, Nolan had worked for the Family in Chicago, as a nightclub manager, utilizing those same organizational abilities of his. He turned a Rush Street dive into a legitimate (if syndicate-owned) money-maker, partially from the local color he provided by serving as his own bouncer. Trouble was, his reputation for being a hardcase fed back into the Family hierarchy and gave some of the top boys the wrong idea: they tried to get Nolan to leave their Rush Street saloon and come in with them, for grooming as a young exec, so to speak, wanting him to start at the bottom in an enforcer capacity. He had balked at the suggestion, and the dispute that caused with the local Family underboss eventually got bloody, and Nolan had to drop out of the Family's sight for a while. "For a while" being almost twenty years, during which he'd turned to heisting. Only recently, when a long-overdue change of regime hit the Chicago Family, had Nolan come into syndicate good graces. Through a lawyer named Felix (the Family *consigliere*), Nolan had been invited in, in the capacity he'd originally sought—nightclub manager—and part-owner as well. The Family offered

Nolan a choice of several multimillion-dollar operations (including a well-known resort and a posh nightclub- cum-restaurant) on the stipulation that he buy in as a partner. That was fine with Nolan, because he had some $400,000 in his friend Planner's safe, his share from the Port City bank job, and this would make an excellent investment for putting the money to use.

Unfortunately, while he was still negotiating with Felix, Nolan's money was stolen and eventually lost, and Nolan was unable to uphold his half of the Family bargain.

And so the Tropical.

The Tropical was a modest operation in comparison with those other places the Family had offered him and, in fact, was used as a trial-run spot for people being considered for top managerial positions in the countless hotels, resorts, niteries and other such establishments owned by the powerful Chicago syndicate. The Tropical was a motel, consisting of four buildings with sixteen units each; two heated swimming pools, one indoor, one out; and a central building housing a restaurant and bar, both of which sported a pseudo-Caribbean decor meant to justify the motel's name. It was located ten miles outside of Sycamore, Illinois, and was devoted to serving honeymooning couples, some of whom were actually married. Lots of legit businessmen out of Chicago, as well as Family people, used it as a trysting ground, and so, accordingly, the Tropical made damn good money for its size.

Nolan himself had been serving a trial run at the Tropical before his money was stolen; now he was there on a more permanent basis, to observe the progress of others undergoing trial runs, doing little more than watching, really—just some mental note-taking and reporting back to Felix on the behavior and capability of the temporary managers. He would break in each new man (whose stay would range from three to six months) and see to it that a sense of continuity was maintained in between these pro tempore managers.

Which meant he mostly sat around.

And considering the salary he was drawing, that didn't make for such a bad setup. At least, not when Sherry was around.

Sherry was young, almost obscenely young, a pretty blonde child who spent most of her time in and out of bikinis. She had applied for a waitress job at the beginning of Nolan's stay at the Tropical, but she couldn't keep the food and coffee out of customer laps, and rather than fire her, Nolan found a place for her. The place was between the sheets of his bed, and when she wasn't there, she was adding to the Tropical's already erotic atmosphere by sunning in her hint of a bikini around the outdoor pool. She was not a brilliant girl, nor was she an empty-headed one, and if she did talk a trifle much, he'd gotten used to it quickly; anyway, her voice was melodious and soothing, so if you didn't listen to the words, it was no trouble at all.

Now she was gone.

The summer was over and there was no sun for her to lie under. She'd begun to get itchy at the tail end of September, and yesterday, when she got the call from her father saying her mother was sick, she'd decided to go back to Ohio and help out her folks. She and Nolan had had their most emotional night last night: she crying and Nolan making an honest effort to be cheerful and kind about the whole thing. She swore she'd come back the next summer; Nolan didn't mention that he hoped to be long gone from the Tropical by then. He just nodded and eased back up on top of her again.

He tried to bank the one ball in and missed. He said, "Shit," and chalked up his cue.

"Want some company?"

"No," Nolan said. He shot again; this time the ball went in.

"Hey. I said, want some company?"

"No," Nolan said.

The kid doing the asking was maybe eighteen, skinny, with long, greasy hair and a complexion like a runny pizza. A fat kid, older by a couple years probably, came sliding up to the table like a hog to slaughter. The skinny kid had on jeans and a gray work shirt with a white patch on the breast pocket that identified the shirt's origin as Ron's Skelly Station and the kid's name as Rick; the fat kid had on a yellow short-sleeve shirt with grease stains and massive underarm sweat-circles, and the buttons over his belly couldn't button.

"Hey, Chub," Rick said to his friend. They were like two balloons, one with the air let out, the other inflated to bursting. "You know what feeling I got about this guy, Chub? I got this awful feeling he's some kind or prick or something." There was emphasis on the word "prick."

Chub, however, said nothing. He just stood there, shifting his weight, from foot to foot and looking Nolan over.

Rick went on. "I mean, I ask him does he want some company and he says, 'shit no.' He's some kind of antisocial bastard, I think. What do you think, Chub?"

Chub, apparently, didn't know what to think. He'd come over to have a laugh with ol' Rick, but now that he was here and had a look at Nolan, he wasn't sure he liked what he saw. After a moment he tapped his skinny friend on the shoulder and gave him a flick of the head that said, come on, don't mess with this dude.

But then reinforcements arrived: two older guys, looking like something out of a fifties hot rod movie, came up from the other end of the hall to see what was the hassle. One of them actually had on a T-shirt with the sleeves rolled up and a cigarette pack stuffed in at the shoulder; he was an emaciated sort with pipe-cleaner arms down under the rolled sleeves, who made the skinny Rick look healthy. His cohort, however, was more genuinely menacing: a sandy-haired, greasy-haired, wide-shouldered bear with close-set, glittering eyes; he wore jeans and a T-shirt under a black cotton vest, and had biceps the size of California grapefruit.

"Okay," Nolan said. "Who wants to play some eightball?"

He played once with Rick and lost. His mind was still elsewhere. But the crowd around began making snide remarks about his shooting, and it brought his mind into focus. When he played the fat kid, for a five, he broke and didn't sink any; then next time his turn came around, he sank all the little-numbered balls and the eight, leaving Chub's stripes scattered all over the table. A murmur went through the small crowd, and pipe-cleaner arms stepped up, and Nolan took five from him the same way. He did it to all of them, except that most times he was running the balls right from the break.

He was good at pool; he was, in fact, good at most games. He'd been playing in a low-stakes poker game regularly with some Sycamore businessmen and had found it an enjoyable enough time killer. Good as he was at games, he was not a gambler. He was interested in pool and card playing for the chance to exercise his mind and to hone his skill; he didn't like to play with pros, because they had their life in the game, and you don't want to screw around with people in something they make a living at. The best amateur doesn't want to play the worst pro, because the game is a lark to the amateur, whereas the pro is deadly serious, and sometime you'll find yourself with a broken head and stuffed in a garbage can if you fuck with the pros and win.

Also, Nolan never hustled. Pool or cards or anything. He could go into a pool hall like this one and almost always clean the place out, if he felt like it; same with lots of small-town, high-stakes card games. But you made enemies that way. Same as when you diddled the pros, the amateur who thinks he's a pro can get pretty mad himself.

Like this crowd around him was now.

"Some kind of smart-ass hustler, buddy? That what you are?" It was the first kid, Rick—skinny Rick with the bad complexion. "Come in here and shoot real shitty and say you don't want to play, and then when we beg you, you say okay and wipe our butts, is that it?"

The bear with the close-set eyes, who seemed to be the leader of this small-time pack, said, "Just lay our money on the table, hustler. Just lay what you stole from us on the table, and you can walk out of here with your ass."

Nolan glanced over toward the proprietor, who was standing by the counter where he served up beers. The proprietor was an elderly guy with a flannel shirt and baggy pants and apron on. He was aware of what was going on, but knew he couldn't do anything about it; these were his usual customers, and he was looking the other way, toward some tables down at the other end of the room, which nobody was using right now.

Nolan picked up the cue ball and threw it at the bear and hit him in the middle of his forehead and knocked him on his back, knocked him out. He used the butt of the cue on Rick's stomach, and Rick promptly crawled away and threw up for a while. The rest of them just stood there and looked at Nolan. Nolan was smiling. And then he saw in their eyes that they realized he wanted them to continue the brawl.

Because Nolan was bored, and hostile, and it was something to do.

Disgusted with himself, Nolan threw the cue down across the table, said, "Fuck it," and walked out of the place. In an hour he was back in his room at the Tropical, fixing himself a shot of Scotch over ice and turning on the news to catch the sports.

At eleven, he was taking a shower and the phone rang.

"Logan?"

It was Sherry. The image of her face flashed through his mind: gentle, little-girl features framed by arcs of blonde-frosted brunette hair . . .

"Where you calling from, Sherry?"

"Home. Ohio. I miss you."

"Yeah. I'm stir-crazy myself, in this room alone."

"My mother's real sick, Logan."

Logan was the name she knew him by, the one he was using at the Tropical.

"Logan?" she said again. He'd been quiet for a moment, his mind full of her naked: her skin coppery from all that summer sun, except for the stark white where the bikini had half-heartedly covered the best parts, the breasts tipped as deep a copper as the sun-tanned skin; the light brunette triangle forming a similar contrast below . . .

"Yeah, I'm here," he said. "I'm sorry to hear your mother's sick."

"She's going to be bedridden a long time."

"I'm sorry."

"I got a job today."

"What kind?"

"Waitress."

"Oh, Christ."

She laughed. "I'll be careful. I haven't scalded anybody's nuts with hot-coffee-in-the-lap yet."

"Oh, then all your customers were women today, huh?"

She laughed some more and then said, "I miss you."

"You said that."

"I know. I want to see you again, Logan."

"Sure. Next summer."

"I don't think you'll still be there. At the Tropical, I mean. You been restless lately."

"Well."

"Let me give you my address. Come and see me when you can. Tell me where you end up, if you end up anywhere."

"I'd like that, Sherry."

She gave him the address, and he wrote it down.

"Logan?"

"Yeah?"

"Take care of yourself. Be happy."

"You too, kid."

They hung up.

Nolan sat there, dripping wet from the shower, getting the bed damp, feeling pissed off and, dammit, lonely. He couldn't understand it, because he'd been self-sufficient for a lot of years, hadn't ever been one to shack up with a broad for more than a day or two.

But he was fifty, and this goddamn life at the Tropical was goddamn getting him down.

He sat there a while and the phone rang again. It was Jon. Calling long-distance from Iowa City.

"Nolan? You got to come here, right away."

Life pumped into his veins; he didn't know what Jon wanted, but whatever it was, Nolan was game.

3

BREEN NEVER THOUGHT it would come to this. Stealing nickels and dimes. Christ! He pulled into the driveway of the little farmhouse where old Sam Comfort and his son Billy were waiting. At least this would end it, he thought. He would be glad to be done with this one; it certainly hadn't been the normal sort of heist he worked. In fact, it hadn't been one heist at all, but a series of thousands of little ones, infinitesimal heists, nickel-and-dime stuff. Literally. Because Breen had been helping the Comforts heist parking meters.

He was a stocky guy of forty-two, black hair cut military-short, his fleshy cheeks covered with a perpetual five o'clock shadow. His eyes were wide-set and dark blue, his nose bumpy and squat in the middle of a rough but intelligent face. Right now, as he sat in his battered green Mustang in the farmhouse drive, Breen's often intense features were softened in pleasant anticipation of severing the alliance with the Comforts.

He guessed he'd been lucky till now. Before this, he'd worked with only the best people; never before had he stooped to the level of the Comforts. He was spoiled, he supposed, from years of working with guys the caliber of Nolan. Used to be, Breen would work at least one job a year with Nolan, picking up one or two more with somebody else reliable. But Jack Taylor and a whole string of good men got busted two summers ago heisting an art gallery, and last year Laughlin and three others were killed after that Georgia armored-car job went sour and they'd been caught between state and local cops in a back-roads chase that turned fucking tragic. Worst of all, about two years ago this time, Breen had been in Chicago with Nolan and several others, planning a bank heist, when some syndicate guy shot the job right out from under them. Word got out later that though Nolan wasn't dead after all (surprising, as that syndicate guy nailed him a couple times; Breen had seen it happen), the Chicago Family was definitely declaring open season on Nolan. Which made it less than healthy to keep company with the man. So what was a guy to do? You had to work with somebody. And if you were desperate enough, you worked with the likes of the Comforts.

Old Sam Comfort's reputation was bad; it went back years before Breen had gotten into the business, and he'd never heard any specific stories about the old man, just that Sam Comfort was not to be trusted. In recent years Sam had worked strictly with his two sons, Billy and Terry, but last year Terry drew a short term for statutory rape, and the Comforts had been lacking a man on their string. And according to Morris (a pawn shop fence in Detroit, whom Breen used as a sort of underworld messenger service), the Comforts had a racket going that required a minimum of three, and they'd been using a fill-in man for Terry Comfort but weren't satisfied with him. Morris suggested that Breen go see the Comforts.

Breen would've dropped the whole thing right there, would've read the handwriting on the wall and just got the hell out of heisting, but he needed the money too bad. Breen was from Indianapolis, where he had a little bar he owned and operated with the help of his wife and brother-in-law. He would've made a good enough living with just the bar, but he was a horse-player; Breen played the horses like an alcoholic drinks and a nymphomaniac screws: in dead earnest, with little joy and less success. He was trying to give it up, but he was into his bookie for four gee's worth of markers, and there was the alimony and child support for his first wife, that blood-sucking bitch; he was way behind on that, and wouldn't it be shit if *that* was the way he finally ended up in stir.

So he'd left the bar in the hands of his wife and brother-in-law and gone to see the Comforts. It was almost a whirlwind trip: when Sam explained they were heisting parking meters, Breen damn near left without sitting down.

But the parking meter deal wasn't as ridiculous as it first sounded. Old Sam had done his homework, no question about it. He'd put together a route: Des Moines, Cedar Rapids, and the Quad Cities, all linked by Interstate 80. He'd spent time in each town tracking prowl car runs, and pinpointed the most untraveled, poorly lit streets, and such prime targets as waterfront parking lots and parking ramps, with thousands of meters for the picking, virtually unattended in the pre-dawn morning hours. He had keys to open the meters, and son Billy (decked out in olive-green uniform with the words "Meter Maintenance" stitched across the back) would go about draining the meters, while Sam stayed around the corner in the car, motor going, Citizen Band radio on to monitor the cops. Breen's role was to empty the buckets of coins that Billy brought him and hand him back a fresh one; Breen would pour the coins into a large, rubber-lined metal tray built down in the floor of the trunk. A lid flopped down over the tray when the night's work was done, a false bottom that made this trunk look like any other in a Buick Electra. No one questioned the maintenance man working the meters (traffic was slow in the wee hours), and most people probably just went by muttering, "Always wondered when they emptied those damn things."

Even with cities as small as those that comprised the Iowa-Illinois Quad Cities, they could pick up several thousand a night, easy, and that was playing it Sam's safe, cagey way, leaving enough coins in each meter to fool the actual maintenance people. That way they could go back for more periodically, and no one would be the wiser, not till the monthly tally for meter earnings came in. Even then, the city might not figure it out: maybe meter revenue was just down that month, who could say?

Sam and Billy rented a house on the outskirts of Iowa City, because it was midway along their Interstate 80 route, but Breen didn't choose to join them. The old man was a boozer and the kid blew grass all the time, and Breen preferred his own company. He chose to stay in Cedar Rapids, where he found an apartment and, before long, a young cocktail waitress to shack up with.

Working with the Comforts had been a royal pain. Not only had the work been hard and tedious, hitting a different city six nights a week for a solid month, but the Comforts had personalities that put a burr up Breen's ass. Billy was an introspective, cynical type, and his old man was an egotistical, egocentric loudmouth, and Breen was glad that most of the time he spent with them was on the job, where keeping quiet was a necessity. Listening to Billy's occasional sarcasm and Sam's constant bullshit was trouble enough on the ride down from Iowa City; at least when the team worked Cedar Rapids, he didn't have to ride in the car with them.

But he had to hand it to old Sam. He'd underestimated the crafty old coot. Sam had the operation down pat, slicker than shit. The Comforts had worked the parking meter scan for a straight year now, alternating between six routes Sam worked out, never staying in one area longer than a month, keeping the local authorities confused. Sam had an account in a bank in each area he hit, but not in any city on the route (he had an account in Iowa City, for example) and used a fictitious name and fictitious business, of course, to keep the bank free of suspicion regarding the heavy amount of coin involved. In Iowa City, Sam posed as the owner of a pinball rental outfit, so the tellers were used to seeing him haul in sacks of coin for deposit. This was canny: others might have fenced the coin at a loss; not old Sam.

Also, Sam had told Breen that he closed out a route after hitting an area a certain number of times; this was the third go-round for the Iowa Interstate 80 route, and it would not be used again, not for several years, anyway. He would develop a new route in untapped territory and add it to his list. And he would be closing out his account at the local bank. This time, the month of meter lootings had tallied $47,000; he had another $110,000 in the Iowa City bank from the other two times he'd hit the area.

Tonight was the payoff. Breen would receive just under twelve thou for his month of hardass work. The $47,000 would be split four ways, with Sam taking a double cut because the package had been put together by the old man. That was fair, Breen thought, and though $12,000 was hardly the best he'd ever done in a heist, it would be enough to get him out of the woods with his bookie and his alimony-hungry ex-wife. Now, if he could just stay away from the damn nags.

He approached the farmhouse, a ramshackle clapboard the Comforts had picked up for cheap rent, not unlike the equally run-down farmhouse outside Detroit, where the

Comforts actually lived, a sprawling shack filled with luxurious possessions bought with the spoils of Comfort heisting. Bunch of slobs, Breen thought, glad tonight would be the end of 'em.

"Come on in, Breen," Sam said, standing in the doorway, framed in light. "Come get your cut." The white-haired, pot-bellied old sot was wearing a green cotton sportcoat with patched elbows over a T-shirt showing the brown suspender straps holding up the baggy brown pants; the old man needed a shave and stood there scratching his ass in the doorway. Fucking slob, Breen thought. Somewhere in the house, the kid would be sitting in his underwear sucking up weed. Nice family.

Breen approached Sam, bracing himself for the blast of whiskey breath, heading up the slanted cement walk toward the house and saying, "After tonight, I'm out, Sam. I've had it; this meter bit is not my bag. You're going to have to add somebody different to the string after tonight."

"Fine with me," Sam said, jovial. "Terry'll be out of stir next month, and we were going to ask you out anyway." They were about ten feet apart. Sam's hand moved out from behind him, where he'd seemed to be scratching his ass, and something glittered in the light coming from inside the house.

Gun metal.

Breen rolled to the left, tumbling on the grass, but old Sam's shot caught him anyway. More gun-fire broke the solitude of the Iowa country evening, explosions as terrifying to Breen as nuclear war. Breen was almost back to his car when another slug caught him in the leg. No matter. He scrambled behind the wheel anyway, ignoring the gunfire behind, ignoring the pain. The back windshield shattered into a sudden spiderweb with a hole punched in its middle, and he felt one of the back tires sag flat.

But he made it out of there. He drove the half-mile into Iowa City, not even looking behind him to see if the Comforts were following. He knew he could lose them; he'd been in Iowa City before and could wind through streets and confuse them. He did that, though he had no idea if they were back there or not. He was getting delirious. He looked down at himself and he was all bloody.

Then he remembered Planner.

That was why he'd been to Iowa City before. To see Planner, that old guy at the antique shop who put together most of Nolan's packages. He could go there for help. He could go see Planner.

He got there, somehow, and stumbled up to the side of the shop and slammed his fist against the door, slammed his fist against the wood again and again, hard as hell, as much to stay awake and keep some sensation going in his body as to rouse somebody inside.

Finally somebody answered. A wild-haired hippie kid, and Breen's hopes sunk in his chest. He mumbled something, like who the hell was this kid, and dropped to the floor just inside the door.

4

THIS WAS ONE of those rare times when all the Charles Atlas muscle-building came in handy. Jon was carrying the bleeding man like an absurdly oversize babe in arms. The guy was heavier than Jon and a shade taller too, and so made quite a load. Jon hauled the fleshy freight to his room in the rear of the shop, hoping that following his impulse to help the guy wasn't some gross error in judgment. Anytime something like this came up, Jon wished he had Nolan around to check with, to consult.

But Nolan isn't here, Jon thought, *so screw wishful thinking.*

As he carried the man, Jon looked him over carefully, trying to get past that first impression of a guy covered with blood. The man was in his early forties, Jon estimated; he had short dark hair, and wore a light blue sportshirt, bloodstained on the lower right side, and summery white slacks, also stained with blood down the left lower leg. The blood on his face apparently had gotten there when a hand had touched one or both of the wounds, and speckles and smears of blood were spread variously around his clothing in spots other than those immediately around the wounds. Jon eased him onto the bed, went upstairs, and came back down with some bandage makings, a bottle of hydrogen peroxide, a basin of water, and several washcloths.

The wounds weren't bad, really. Not near as bad as he'd at first thought, from the shock of the blood-soaked clothes; it was the light colors that made the red stand out so, the light blue shirt and white pants, and the guy must've run after he was shot, scattering blood around on his clothes. Jon was relieved to find the leg just nicked, and the side wound showed evidence of the bullet going through clean, nothing important having been hit. Or that was Jon's guess, anyway; if the slug had caught an artery there'd be blood gushing everywhere, but the bleeding here wasn't severe at all. Jon washed the wounds clean and applied bandages that were tight, but not tourniquet-tight.

The guy came around just as Jon was finishing.

He said, "Who . . . who the hell are you?"

"You asked that before," Jon said. "Suppose you tell me

who the hell you are, and we'll see about who I am afterwards."

"Where's Planner?"

Jon's suspicions were confirmed: this was an associate of his late uncle, someone who'd run into trouble on a heist or something and had come here for help. That had been Jon's first guess, and as he'd been in a similar boat that time with Nolan, his instinct had been to help this man.

"I said, where's Planner, kid? You do know who I'm talking about?"

"I know who you're talking about," Jon said. Then, after a moment, "Planner was my uncle."

"Was?"

"He's dead. Few months now."

"Jesus." The guy propped himself up on his elbows and spoke, almost to himself. "Jesus Christ, these days everybody good's either dead or in jail, seems like. . . . Jesus H. Christ. How'd it happen, anyway?"

Jon started to hesitate again, but those last comments from the guy sounded right, so he said, "My uncle was keeping money in his safe for some people. Two men came in and took the money and killed him."

"Shit! Is that right? Shit. Somebody ought to find those guys and . . ."

"Somebody did. You feeling okay? You look kind of pale. You better lay back and take it easy."

"I feel okay."

"Yeah, well, I don't think your wounds are too serious, but you better lay back and take it easy just the same."

"I appreciate this, kid, you taking me in, patching me up like this."

"If you appreciate it so damn much, you might tell me who you are and what's going on."

"Well, I'm in the business your uncle was in. You know what sort of business your uncle was in, don't you, kid?"

"I do. I'm in that line of work myself."

"Antiques, you mean? Like all this old comic book bullshit you got in here?"

"You know what I mean."

"Okay, then. So who have you worked with, if that's the line of work you're in."

"Nolan. He's the only one so far. Him and some people you wouldn't know."

"I thought Nolan had Family troubles."

"Not anymore."

"You worked with Nolan? What, on your first job? What'd he want to screw around with a goddamn kid like you for? No offense."

"Because big-deal pros like you wouldn't come near him. No offense. That Family trouble, remember?"

The guy was convinced. He said, "My name is Breen," and held out his hand, which Jon shook; for a guy just shot, Breen had a hell of a grip. "An old whoremonger named Sam Comfort and his pothead kid Billy just pulled a double-cross, with me on the shitty end of the stick. I wouldn't be talking about it right now if the senile old fart hadn't been half crocked when he started shooting."

Jon had never heard of the Comforts. He said so.

"Well, you're lucky. They aren't a family, they're a social disease." He sat up again, quickly. "Hell! Listen, you better move my car. I left it outside, and the Comforts know about Planner and might figure I came here. You got a gun? I don't carry one, goddamn it, or I might've stayed there and shot it out with the fuckheads. But you better get a gun and go out there and move that goddamn car of mine, the windshield's shot to shit, and if nothing else, you don't want some cop spotting it and asking questions."

"Okay," Jon said.

"*Do* you have a gun, kid?"

"I got a couple."

"Maybe I ought to back you up. Maybe you ought to help me out of this bed, and I'll stand at the window or something and back you up . . ."

"Look. Lean back and shut up. For a guy just got shot, you're sure lively. If you don't talk yourself to death, you'll do it to me."

"Say," Breen said. "You do know Nolan, don't you?"

Jon grinned, told the guy to shut up and rest, and left him.

Back upstairs, Jon stuck one of his uncle's .32 automatics in his waistband, threw on a wind- breaker, and went down to move the car. First he drove his own car, an old Chevy II he'd had for some time, out of the garage in the rear and re-placed it with Breen's Mustang. Then he shut the garage door and pulled the nose of the Chevy II up just close to touching. The door had no windows, and the way the garage was built into the shop's back end, it had windows on the left side only, and those were opaque and grilled, with no way for anyone to see whether or not the Mustang was in there, short of breaking in. Not that breaking in didn't sound like something the Comforts were easily capable of.

He was just inside the door when light came shooting through one of the side windows in the shop, the lights from the front beams of a car pulling in. The Comforts had come calling. He took the windbreaker off and stuck the .32 in his belt behind his back, leaving right hand on hip for easy access.

The knock came soon enough, and Jon sucked in wind. He told himself to be calm, damn it, calm, and wondered if once, just once, he could pull off something without Nolan holding his hand. There was a night latch on the door, which Jon left bolted, cracking open the door to stare into a gray-eyed, wrinkled old face that had to belong to Sam Comfort. It was the sort of face that looked kind, superficially, but actually was full of the smile-lines that come from a sadistic sense of humor. Sixty-some years ago, you would've found this man a child, pulling the wings off butterflies.

"Who the hell are you?" Sam Comfort asked.

Jon was getting tired of that question. On top of his case of nerves, it was especially irritating, and he moved his right hand further back on his hip, closer to the .32, rubbing the sweat off his palm as he did. He said, "It's after midnight, mister. We're closed."

Comfort's boozy breath was overpowering, but the gray eyes were not unclear; he was the type of man who could drink you under the table and not feel it himself.

He said, "I'm not a customer."

'That makes us even," Jon said, "because I'm not selling anything."

"I'm an old friend of Planner's."

"I don't care what you are," Jon said, and started to close the door.

Thick, strong fingers curled around the door's edge and held it open. "I said I'm a friend of Planner's. Tell him an old friend's here to see him."

"Let go of the door."

Comfort did, tentatively.

Jon said, "My uncle—Planner—is dead."

"Oh, I'm sorry. Sorry. I hadn't heard. How did it happen, boy?"

"Heart attack." Which was what the death certificate had said, anyway, and an expensive damn piece of paper that was, too.

"And you're his nephew, then? Taking over the business, are you?"

"No. I got no interest in antiques, and I'm going to sell all the stock at once, soon as a good buyer turns up, and will you please get out of here and let me get some sleep?"

The gray eyes narrowed, then eased up. "Well, I'm sorry to see you so hostile to an old friend of your uncle's, and I'm sorry to hear the news about his untimely end. Please accept my condolences."

"Sure. Sorry if I was short."

"Understandable. Say, what you keep in that garage of yours?"

"If it was a garage, I'd keep my car in it. But it isn't, it's a storeroom. Good night."

And he pushed the door shut and locked it, and stepped to one side in case any bullets should come flying through. Several heartbeats later, he crept to the side window and looked out to see the old man join a long-haired kid, leaning up against their Buick Electra. They shared a few moments of heated conversation, most of the heat coming from the old man, as the kid was a spacey type. Then both men shrugged. The old man got behind the wheel, the kid next to him, and they drove away.

When he rejoined Breen, the man was asleep and snoring. Jon was at first relieved that he wouldn't have to listen to any more of the talkative man's ramblings, but then he thought better of it, shook the guy awake, and told him about the brush with the Comforts.

"You're okay, kid," Breen said, grinning. "You handled old Sam beautiful, sounds like."

"Why don't you show your gratitude," Jon said, "by telling me what all this is about."

Breen did. He told Jon he'd been working a month of parking meter heists ("Small potatoes, kid, but over the long haul, she adds up!"); told him old man Comfort had over a hundred and fifty gees, cash, from several such runs of meter heisting in the area, and had tried to kill Breen less than an hour earlier, to avoid paying Breen's $12,000 share.

"Listen," Jon said. "I'm going to call Nolan. I think maybe he'll have some ideas concerning the Comforts."

Breen thought that was fine.

Jon went out to the phone that sat on the long counter behind which Planner had constantly sat puffing expensive cigars. Jon sat on the counter, dialing the phone, thinking of his uncle's violent death, wondering if he was being a fool to follow in those bloody footsteps. But he forgot that when he heard Nolan's, "Yeah?"

"Nolan? You got to come here, right away."

"What's the problem, kid?" Nolan's voice was calm, but Jon seemed to detect a note of enthusiasm in it.

"You know a guy named Breen?"

"I do."

Jon filled Nolan in on what had happened to Breen, and how he'd come bleeding up to Jon's doorstep.

"What about a doctor?"

"I bandaged him up, Nolan. He'll last okay. Maybe tomorrow we can get Doc Ainsworth in for a look at him. So far, I been more concerned about the Comforts than anything."

"Rightly so. And you were right not bringing in a doctor, because the Comforts might be watching. You locked the doors, of course? And moved Breen's car?"

"Of course. And the Comforts have already come around

once." He'd held that back to shock Nolan with—saved it for effect.

But he should have known better with Nolan, who just said an emotionless, "Well?"

And Jon told him about the run-in with Sam Comfort.

"You're doing better all the time, kid. In fact, what do you need me for there? You got things under control."

"Well, for one thing, these damn Comforts got me sweating. They're unpredictable, judging from what Breen says, and from what I saw of them."

"Did you fool old Sam, you think?"

"I got an idea what was going on in that head. He could come barging in with a gun right now and I wouldn't be surprised. You know the Comforts pretty well, Nolan?"

"I worked a job with that crusty old son of a bitch, years ago. He didn't cross me, because I didn't give him the opening. But if my back had been to him, he'd have put the knife in, no doubt about it. Breen was stupid to work with him in the first place. Everybody knows Sam is as crazy as he is unreliable."

"Well, Nolan, what do you think?"

"I'll come, yeah."

"It's not that I need help, exactly . . ."

"I know, kid. You just like having me around."

"That's part of it."

"And that hundred and fifty thousand of Comfort's is another."

"Right."

"We're about due, Jon. Maybe we can help my old buddy Breen and do ourselves a favor, too."

Jon grinned into the phone. "Right."

Two

———

5

THE RIOTS COULD have been last week, the way this neighborhood looked. Buildings stood black and gutted from flames; no one had even bothered boarding up the broken-out, blown-out windows, which stared from the buildings like the empty sockets of gouged-out eyes. Other blocks had fared better, their buildings untouched by flame, some stores none the worse for wear, open for business. But even these more fortunate blocks showed the scars of violence, their wounds no less ugly for the pus being dried up and crusted over. The sites of many small businesses were vacant now, abandoned by their white proprietors in the wake of black unrest, leaving behind storefront windows broken out and never replaced, nothing remaining but jagged edges of glass, like teeth in the mouth of a screaming man. Outrage had fired this violence, from which had come further outrage: one emigrant had boarded up his storefront window and written, in an angry red scrawl: "AFTER 20 YRS. SERVICE, CHASED FROM OUR HOME," a star of David beneath the words like a signature. Passing by the boarded-up store was a thin black woman in a pale, worn, green dress, trudging along like a parody of a weary darkie, pulling a child's wagon filled with groceries, and her face told the whole story: she'd had to walk blocks and blocks to a grocery store, and hoped like hell nothing spoiled. She seemed to shake her head a little as she moved along past her neighborhood corner grocery, which was an empty, burned-out shell.

Nolan sat in the back of the taxi cab, listening to the meter tick his money away, and half listening to the cabbie, who'd been pointing out the sights like a cynical tour guide. The cabbie had grown up in this part of Detroit himself and was saddened and somewhat pissed off about what had happened here since he'd left it for a better neighborhood.

Back at the airport, Nolan had chosen this black cabbie over a white one, because he wasn't sure if the white cabbie would've wanted to drive him into this neighborhood. Matter of fact, Nolan was a little ill at ease himself; he'd feel a hell of a lot better armed, but he hadn't been able to carry heat on the plane because of skyjacking precautions. He'd brought a gun along, of course, a pair of them in fact: two S & W .38s with four-inch barrels. But they were packed away in his suitcase (no sweat from airport security on that—only hand-carried bags routinely got checked), and a .38 nestling between his fresh socks and change of underwear wouldn't do him much good down here. The suitcase, and Jon, ought to be at the hotel by now; this taxi ride had been one that Nolan felt better taken alone, so he'd sent the kid on ahead with the luggage on the airport-to-hotel shuttle bus.

Which was considerably cheaper than this damn taxi, but then, you didn't find a shuttle running from airport to ghetto and had to expect to pay the price. The price in this case was double stiff: the tinny racket of that disembodied mechanical head hooked to the dash, wolfing down Nolan's money, was depressing enough, let alone having to put up with the cabbie's gloomy line of patter.

The cabbie was a thickset, very black man with white hair and white mustache, and was maybe a year or two older than Nolan. "Yessir," the cabbie was saying (*why couldn't I get a sullen one*, Nolan thought, *or at least one of those mumble-mouths you can't make heads or tails of*), "this neighborhood was hit super-bad, rioting and lootings and snipings and you name it. Bad hit as any place in the country."

Nolan grunted, to show he was paying attention. He glanced at the meter and winced: attention wasn't all he was paying—fourteen bucks and climbing. Christ!

The cabbie rambled on. "Martin Luther King weren't the only thing got killed, that time. This whole neighborhood went down with him. Look at it. You ever seen a place so tore-up?"

"No," Nolan said, though it wasn't true. Berlin had been like this, after the war.

"You know, where I'm taking you, it's about the only business in the area didn't get hurt. All them cars, and not even a antenna busted off. And a white fella runs it, can you beat that?"

"No."

"Huh?"

"No, I can't beat that."

Nolan's lack of interest finally dawned on the guy, and shut him up. Which was no big deal, as they were within a block of Bernie's Used Auto Sales anyway.

Bernie's was indeed a white man's business that had gone untouched in the rioting, and with half a block of cars sitting out in the open like that, it was a wonder. The big garage next to the lot had gone untouched as well, not even a broken pane of glass. It was not hard to figure: Bernie's business was not one the neighborhood would like to lose. A grocery store was expendable, but not Bernie's.

Nolan got out of the taxi, looked at the meter, which read "$15.50." He handed the cabbie a twenty and waited for change, but the guy just grinned, said "Thanks," and roared off. Nolan now understood how the cabbie had made it to a better neighborhood.

Immediately, a salesman approached Nolan, saying, "What can we do for you, my man?" His words were mild enough, but his tone and expression said, *What the fuck you doin' here, whitey?* He was a lanky, chocolate-colored guy who couldn't keep still. Nolan hated goddamn funky butts like this; he liked people who didn't move anything but their mouths when they talked, and not much of that. This guy was a fluid son of a bitch poured into a white-stitched black suit and a wide-brimmed gangster hat. The band was wide and black, the hat itself white, and Nolan had seen George Raft in a similar one, years ago. It looked better on Raft.

"Tell Bernie I'm here."

The guy stopped dancing, narrowed his eyes on Nolan. "Uh, like who should I say . . ."

"Tell him Nolan."

"He's not . . . "

"He's expecting me. Didn't he tell you? No, I don't suppose he would. Tell him."

The guy's eyes filled with something, and it wasn't love. "Okay," he said. "Wait here till I see if it's cool with the man."

"Okay."

The salesman strode off, but his butt seemed slightly less funky now. His reaction to Nolan had been a natural one, as most of Bernie's white customers never showed their faces around here, making arrangements to see Bern at his suburban home or at one of his junkyards. Nolan walked around the lot while he waited, taking a look at Bernie's stock.

The lot was packed with cars, of recent vintage mostly, every make and model from Volks to Mercedes, Pinto to Caddy. An impressive selection, but to the casual observer, nothing unusual. Nolan was not a casual observer, and he was smiling, thinking of the one thing that separated Bernie's from your run-of-the-mill used-car lot: virtually every car on the well-stocked lot was a stolen one.

But the skill and workmanship of Bernie and staff saw to it that every car sold off the lot was not only untraceable, but offered to the public at bargain pricing and with full warranty. This was why Bernie's had been an oasis in a desert of rioting: nobody kills the golden goose, and Bernie was him, Bernie was the goose who'd provided this neighborhood with countless golden eggs. Rip off a car in the morning, and by early afternoon Bern's cash was in your pocket, and Bern was cool, he paid off fair, no hassle, no shuck. And on top of being where you could unload the car you stole for ready cash, Bernie's was a mother of a cheap place to buy wheels. If there was one white dude in the neighborhood who deserved being called brother, it was Bern, baby, Bern.

Nolan wasn't precisely sure how Bernie worked this gig, but he did know that Bernie had been a jump-title expert for years. Last Nolan knew, Bernie owned a chain of junkyards all over the Detroit area and, by matching up stolen cars with junked cars of the same make, he simply spot-welded the junker's serial numbers onto the stolen job—under the hood, inside the door and, when possible, on the frame—and presto, a "new" car ready for titling. Legislation had, in recent years, crippled jump-title rackets badly, especially on the large scale that Bernie worked; but fortunately, a southern state notorious for its lax titling laws was glad to have Bernie's trade, and the particular county Bernie did his business through even went so far as to service him by mail-order. Sounded far-fetched, but Nolan remembered the time in Alabama, not so very long ago, when he'd stolen a car and, with no proof of ownership whatever, driven up to the courthouse, got the auto tided, and driven it away.

"Yer fat!"

Nolan turned, and Bernie was standing there, a short, massively muscled man with not an ounce of flab on him; he had a round face with round eyes and round nose and, when he spoke, a round mouth. If he hadn't had a full head of curly brown hair, he'd have looked like a talking cueball. He was wearing the world's dirtiest coveralls, with "Bernie's" emblazoned over one breast pocket "How'd you get so goddamn fat?"

"I'm an old man, Bernie. I live a soft life these days."

"Soft life, my ass. Come on, Nolan, let's go in the back and have some beer."

Why Bernie didn't have a potbelly from constant beer guzzling was one of the mysteries of life Nolan would never understand. Maybe the man just worked hard enough to offset all those suds: Bernie, never content to live high on the carloads of cash his business brought him, spent most of his time in there doing the drudge work—painting the cars, doing body work, replacing parts, everything. It was obvious that Bernie didn't need to do illegal work to make a good living; but the illegal route had led to his own shop, his own operation, and freedom was always worth a little risk. One thing was for sure, Nolan thought: Bernie ran the most efficient automotive firm in Detroit And probably the most honest.

The back room was a cubbyhole with a small desk and a large cooler of beer. The desk was cluttered with car manuals, the Red and Blue Books of this and many a year, bills and receipts, and so on. Nolan knew the reason for the mess: Bernie kept good books, but felt that overly neat records made the IRS unduly suspicious. Besides, he got a kick out of making them come in and dig. If they wanted to come and look for ways to screw you, cross your legs and make 'em work their asses off getting in.

Bernie popped a top and handed a foaming beer to Nolan, did the same for himself. "So yer fat, and you ain't dead."

"Yes I'm fat, no I'm not dead."

"You already told me why you're fat. Now tell me why you ain't dead."

"Didn't you hear about the change of regime in Chicago?"

"No. I got no Family ties, never did have. I'm an independent and like to stay clear of that shit. You know me, Nolan. So what, the people that wanted you dead, those Family people, are out? And what, the new people love you?"

"Something like that."

"What are you up to now?"

Nolan told Bernie about the Tropical.

"Sounds boring."

"It is. But it's a good deal, for the immediate present, and I don't want to blow it"

"How could you blow it?"

"Well, you see, Bernie, I'm here on business. Detroit's never been my idea of a place to vacation."

"So?"

"The Family people I'm fronting for don't want me straying from the straight and narrow. They got a name and background set up for me, so I can front the Tropical with no static from the law or anybody. Somebody runs a check on me, I sound like the president of the goddamn Chamber of Commerce. Hell, I'm even a college graduate, would you believe that?"

"I believe you can pass for one," Bernie said, getting a fresh beer. "I joined this country club, and it's full of those Phi Beta crappers. They're some of the dumbest, most boring assholes I ever hung around with. If Thelma didn't insist we belong, I'd get the hell out."

Bernie's social-climbing wife, and the indignities he suffered because of her, was a topic Nolan could do without, so he steered around it, saying, "Anyway, Bern, my point is, there are certain of my former activities the Family doesn't want me engaging in."

"Shit, you're even starting to *sound* like a damn college man. Okay, so you're here for a heist. And you want the lid kept on it."

"Right, Bern."

"What do you need, a car? You can have a car as long as you're in town, Nolan. On the house. Course, if you wreck it, I'll expect you to buy the thing. That's only fair, I mean."

"More than fair. But you could help me another way."

"Whatever it is, I'll do what I can."

"I need some supplies for the job. And I figure the less people I talk to, better off I am. Can you get me what I need?"

"Think so. Anything short of a tank, anyway. What is it you want?"

Nolan told him.

"What the hell you need those for?"

"I don't want the guys I'm heisting to see me. If they see me, I'll have to shoot them."

"Getting soft, Nolan? Ain't fat bad enough?"

"I never been one to kill without reason, Bernie." That was true enough, but Nolan didn't go into the rest of it—that his main reason was, he didn't want to subject Jon to violence that extreme. If he could help it.

"Well, okay, Nolan. You always known what you was doing. Sit and have another beer—there's plenty in the cooler. I'll go get a man to rustle that crazy shit up for you. Run you about twenty-five bucks per. What you want, a couple?"

Nolan nodded.

"Okay, good as done. But I were you, I'd remember those toys're no substitute for firepower. You can't beat a gun, no way."

"Oh, I'll have a gun, Bern. I may be getting soft and fat, but I'm not crazy."

6

THE BALLROOM was filled with long tables, tables stacked with the wares of dozens of individual dealers, and hundreds of kids-of-all-ages were filing past the tables, stopping to examine those wares. The dealers ranged from small-time local collectors getting rid of their duplicates, to big-time operators who'd come from either coast in vans loaded with boxes and boxes of rare material. The goods of both were scrutinized with equal suspicion by prospective buyers, who slipped the books from their plastic bags to make sure each was properly graded, fairly priced, going over each yellowing artifact like a jeweler looking for flaws in a diamond. A generally cordial mood reigned, however, and the horse-trading, the bickering over an item's monetary worth, was considerably more amiable than what you might run into at a pawnbroker's, say, or an antique shop. Jon, in his jeans and sweatshirt, fit in well with this crowd, who hardly looked prosperous, unless you noticed that greenbacks of just about every denomination were clutched in the countless hot little hands like so much paper. Though the throng included kids below teen-level, as well as men into middle age and beyond, most were closer to Jon's age, and ran to type: male; glasses; skin problems; skinny (or fat) or short (or tall); ultra-long hair (or ultra-short); T-shirts with super-heroes on them. If Nolan were here, he'd look at this crowd and figure them for the bums of tomorrow—hell, bums of *today*—but in reality these were highly intelligent, if slightly screwball young adults, potential Supermen even if they did look more like offbeat Clark Kents.

What was going on was a comic book convention. This ballroom in a downtown Detroit hotel had been converted into "Hucksters' Hall," and Jon, like all the scruffy fans wandering through the room in search of pulp-paper dreams, was dropping money like a reckless Monopoly player: in his first twenty minutes, Jon passed GO, spent his $200. This is what he purchased: three Big Little Books, two

Flash Gordon, one Buck Rogers; one *Weird Fantasy* comic with a story by Wood; and two *Famous Funnies* comics with old Buck Rogers strips inside and covers by Frazetta. All of it was the comic book version of science fiction; that is, pirates in outer space: Killer Kane hijacking Buck's rocket ship; Ming the Merciless holding Dale Arden captive to lure Flash into a trap; pirates flying the skull-and-crossbones in the sea of outer space. Great stuff.

So why was he so damn unhappy?

Not about the prices he'd had to pay—he'd done all right on the items he picked up so far, by shrewd if halfhearted haggling—and not in disappointment at the size of this convention, though it really didn't compare to the New York Cons, whose Huckster rooms were breathtaking, both in scope and prices. This convention was not, after all, totally devoted to comics, being the Detroit Three-Way Fan-Fare, a joint gathering of comics freaks, science-fiction enthusiasts and old-movie buffs. Since Jon fell into each category, he naturally was more than pleased with the arrangement.

But right now he was feeling low, an exceptional state of affairs considering he was now in the middle of the atmosphere that most nearly fit his conception of heaven: namely, a room full of comic books. Not unhappy exactly, more like unnerved. Moody. Jumpy. Ill at ease.

Tonight—the prospect of tonight—was scaring the bejesus out of him.

When Nolan had suggested going to Detroit and ripping off old man Comfort, the convention came immediately to Jon's mind; but he decided to wait for the right moment to spring the idea on Nolan. When Jon did ask if it was okay if they stayed at this particular hotel, Nolan's left eyebrow had raised and he'd said, "Comic books. It has something to do with comic books . . . I don't know how in hell it can, but it does."

Jon admitted as much, pointing out, "The convention'll get my mind off the job—I won't get all fumble-ass nervous about the thing. You can do your setup work, getting the car and the other stuff, and I can spend the afternoon looking at old comic books. It'll keep my mind from dwelling too much on tonight."

They'd been sitting on the plane at the time, having driven to the Quad City Airport in Moline for a Friday morning flight to Detroit. They hadn't phoned ahead any hotel reservations, as it was Nolan's intention to find a cheap motel once they got there. He'd made the intention known to Jon, who hadn't been surprised by it, considering that right then they'd been sitting in the plane's tourist section, another of Nolan's money-saving tactics. Their conversation had to be couched in euphemisms, as they took up only two of three adjoining seats, the window seat being occupied by a conservatively dressed businessman who might be offended by discussion of the armed robbery pending.

Jon had discovered, through experience, that Nolan was something of a cheapskate. While Nolan had earned some half-million dollars in his fifteen years as a professional thief, he'd kept the bulk of it salted away in banks, while living a painfully spartan existence. Nolan had been satisfied with modest apartments and second-hand Fords because he lived for tomorrow—that is, had planned an early retirement from the heist game, a retirement that would include a nightclub Nolan wanted to own and operate through his "twilight years."

But now that Nolan had been wiped out of his half-million nest egg, not once but *twice* (Jon's along with it, the second time) you'd think the guy would've learned you might as well enjoy yourself today since a safe's liable to fall on you tomorrow.

But no. With Nolan it was tourist-class seats and cheap motels and, Jon supposed, a hamburger joint for supper.

So when Nolan didn't seem to be buying the argument about the hotel with the comics con being a way to keep Jon's mind off the job, Jon mentioned the special room rate; if thrift didn't win Nolan over, nothing would. "We can have a double room for twenty bucks, Nolan. That's less than half price. People attending the convention get the rooms less than half price."

"Okay, kid. Whatever you want."

It pleased him he was finally beginning to find the means to occasionally come out on top with Nolan.

Not that Jon didn't still admire the man. But Nolan's cheapness was at least a chink in the armor; it was nice to know the guy wasn't perfect, that he was human in a few ways, at least. Nicer still was knowing that in the ways that counted—survival, for instance—Nolan was a rock. Jon liked to cling to that rock.

He could've used that rock right now.

Because the convention wasn't proving to have the distracting effect he'd thought it would.

That old man, Sam Comfort, with his spooky gray eyes and sadism-lined face, was a constantly recurring image in Jon's mind, a strong, chilling image that could crowd out even the four-color fantasies strewn out along the dealers' tables in Hucksters' Hall. Tonight. Tonight Jon and Nolan would be going up against that crazy, *crazy* old man, and if all went well, they'd come away with a strongbox full of that senile old bastard's money. Which was dandy, only they hadn't done the thing yet; it lay ahead to be done, tonight.

And Jon was scared shitless at the thought.

He'd been eager at the prospect, sure; he was hot to get back some of that money he'd lost a month- and-a-half ago, and when Nolan outlined the plan to rip off Sam Comfort and Son, it had sounded good to him, and still did. But that was back in Iowa City, in homey, security-lined surroundings, where planning a robbery was like plotting the story of a new comic strip. The execution of the plan seemed light-years away, the hazy end result of a sharp but abstract concept. And this, this was Detroit, they were *here* already, and a few hours from now Jon would be laying his ass on the line.

He'd done it before, of course, laid his ass on the line in one of Nolan's potentially violent undertakings (hell of an unpleasant word, that— undertaking, Jesus!) but that didn't make things any easier. Last year, he'd gone into that first robbery with a very naive sort of attitude, an out-of- focus view, a comic-book idea of action and adventure and derring-do. Then, when everything had turned to shit, guns blasting into people and throwing blood around and turning human beings into limp and lifeless meat, Jon had suddenly realized that Nolan's life was not capes and bullets-bouncing-off, it was the real goddamn thing. The bullets went through you, and blood and bone and stuff came flying out the other side, and afterward, Jon would've been glad to take Nolan's advice to "let this cure you of living out your half-ass fantasies." But no sooner had Nolan got out those words, than the situation erupted into violence once again, and Jon had to respond in kind, had to pull Nolan's ass out of the fire, and get him to where he maybe could be kept alive.

When the cordite fumes had lifted from the situation, when the blood had been cleaned up and the people buried, when the bank robbery and its gory aftermath had fuzzed over in his mind and become just an exciting memory, Jon had been lulled into thinking it had been sort of fun and, after all, he'd come out of it with not a scratch. So he'd fallen into the trap again, equating Nolan's life with goddamn Batman or something, only to be reminded, the hard way, that the game Nolan played was for high stakes, the highest—life or death—not to mention those lesser gambles, getting maimed, maybe, or jailed. He'd been reminded of that when those guys shot his uncle and stole the money and got him back in the thick again. And now, with that nightmare just beginning to fade in his mind, he was suckering himself back into Nolan's precarious lifestyle once more, hopefully to recoup some of the money they'd both lost last go-round.

Not so many hours ago, Jon'd had a talk with Breen, and that talk was lingering in the back of Jon's head, nagging him as much as the image of old man Comfort. Nolan had arrived around two-thirty in the morning and, after a talk with Breen, had driven out to the house on Iowa City's outskirts to see if the Comforts were still around. Nolan figured they wouldn't be, but felt it best to check, and had Jon stay with Breen at the antique shop, armed, in case the Comforts attacked while Nolan was gone.

During that time, while they waited for Nolan's return, Jon and Breen had talked. Breen's first question was, "Are you related to Nolan or something? His fucking bastard kid or something?" Breen seemed slightly irritated.

Jon was taken aback by the question. "Not that I know of. What the hell makes you come up with an idea like that?"

"I don't know," Breen said, shaking his head. "I known Nolan a long time, and I never seen him act like this."

"Like what?"

"He's goddamn pampering you, kid. Isn't like him. You know what he said to me?"

"No." Which was true. Jon had not been a party to Breen and Nolan's conversation.

"He said he had to be careful old man Comfort didn't see who was robbing him! Can you imagine?"

Jon said, "What's wrong with that? Comfort and Nolan know each other, and so of course Nolan doesn't want him to know who's pulling the job."

"Don't you see it? He's puttin' on the kid gloves when he ought be bare-knuckle punchin'. This kind of thing, when you heist another heister, you got to kill the guy. You don't leave people like that alive after ripping 'em off. Not people like Sam Comfort, you don't. Or he'll come around and cut off your dick and feed it to you."

Jon swallowed at that not particularly appetizing thought. "So what?" he said, straining to sound flip. "That .just means Nolan is right—you got to keep Comfort from knowing who it is, otherwise you got a lot of . . . you know, bloodshed on your hands."

Breen sat up in bed, groaning just a little from his gunshot wounds. "Now, I'll admit," he said through tight lips, "I'll admit that Nolan's always been one to avoid killing when he could, but not in a case like this. You got to lance a boil like the Comforts. It's safer all around, just to go in and blow those bastards' heads off and call it a night."

"Big talk, Breen. And you don't even carry a gun."

"Right, I don't, but Nolan does. I wouldn't go for killing the Comforts or anybody, but I wouldn't think of ripping them off, either, not for revenge or nothing. I'm lucky to be out of it with my ass. I'm a coward. Ask Nolan. I ran out on him that time in Chicago, when those syndicate boys shot him up. And that's another reason this thing puzzles me.

Nolan says he's going to give me a share of the take, like he's going after the Comforts as a favor to me. What for? He owes me nothing. I'm lucky he doesn't kick my fuckin' butt in for running the hell out on him that time. So what is it with him? Why's he jumpin' on this like it's his golden opportunity? Why's he a goddamn humanitarian where the Comforts are concerned?"

And at this stage Jon had realized what lay behind Breen's point of view. After the robbery, the Comforts might naturally figure that Breen had had a hand in it, to get back at them for their double-cross and get his due from the parking meter heisting. So of course Breen wanted the Comforts dead; of course he was uneasy about Nolan sparing the lives of that miserable family. Breen himself was the one most likely to (gulp) get his dick cut off and fed to him.

But what Breen said did bother Jon. Was Nolan taking undue risks, to spare Jon? Was Nolan avoiding violence with the Comforts to keep things from getting too rough for Jon? Was Breen right—with people like the Comforts, were you better off just killing them? That final concept was one Jon didn't really think he could stomach. Did Nolan know that, too, Jon wondered?

After spending another hundred bucks, Jon left the Hucksters' Hall and went upstairs to the room he and Nolan would share. It was a dreary cubicle, despite the hotel's lavish lobby, dining area, and bar, and was robbery even at convention rates. He undressed, had a cold shower, and got dressed again and went down to the bar, to have a drink and fog his mind if not clear it.

It was an off-time right now: the bar was part of a big nightclub setup, with stage and arena of tables over to the right, and the room was almost as big as the ballroom where the comic dealing was going on, only this was as empty of people as Hucksters' Hall was full. Up at the bar was a pretty woman with short brown pixie hair. She was wearing slacks and a sweater over a blouse—casual clothes but very stylish, in dark, soft colors: blues, browns. She was thin as a model, but full-breasted. Jon supposed she was in her early thirties, close to Karen's age.

Why did he have to think of Karen at a moment like this? Now, along with all those other bad vibes running through him—fear and depression and edginess—now he felt *guilty*, too. Because he was thinking of going up and sitting next to that woman at the bar, pinning his hopes on the improbable possibility of his picking her up, thinking that maybe a little sex game (even if conversation was as far as it got) would drain off his tension. But, no—just thinking of it made things worse; now he felt guilty for possibly betraying Karen.

Fortunately he was able to brush the guilt quickly from his mind. He just thought about this morning, when he'd called Karen to tell her as tactfully as possible that he would be attending the comics convention, and she'd gone into a fury, a goddamn rage about him missing her birthday for a stupid bunch of comic books. She'd given him no chance to explain (and he couldn't have—Karen knew of Nolan and disapproved of Nolan-sponsored activities even more than she did comic books), and she'd really been quite unreasonable.

So, conscience clear, he sat down next to the pretty brunette and smiled and built a strategy. And when the bartender came around, Jon ordered a Scotch on the rocks for himself (he hated Scotch, but it sounded rugged), and as he turned to her to ask what she'd have, damn if the bartender didn't card him!

His outline for seduction erased itself on his mental blackboard and, as he looked at the beautiful, dark-haired, full-breasted woman in her early thirties sitting next to him, with her finely chiseled features and a smile turning from invitation to condescension, Jon decided not even to bother digging his I.D. out of his wallet, just forgot the Scotch and the woman and got the hell out of there.

He went back up to the cubicle, had another cold shower, and got dressed again and went down and spent another hundred on comic books. It killed the time till he was supposed to meet Nolan in the coffee shop downstairs.

7

NOLAN STEPPED onto the elevator and was all alone, except for a girl with sharply pointed ears and skin tinted a dark green. She was wearing a silver sarong that made her look as though she'd been wrapped in aluminum foil, like a sandwich. She was young, probably sixteen, a chunky but not unattractive girl—considering she was green and had pointed ears.

It was Nolan's sincere hope that she would not be going all fifteen floors down to the lobby, as he was. He'd just come from the hotel room, where he'd found evidence that Jon was developing a cleanliness fetish—the boy apparently had had at least a couple of showers already, as all the towels were used up and the floor was wet. All of which was only in keeping with this nuthouse hotel, this asylum populated by kids so weird, they made Jon seem normal.

Like, for instance, this green, pointy-eared girl with whom he shared the elevator. Nolan hoped she'd get off soon so he wouldn't have to say anything to her. Strangers were always a pain to talk to, let alone green ones. She would ask him if he wondered why she was made up this way, and he would say no, but it would be too late: they would be talking, and this was a particularly slow elevator that could make a fifteen-floor ride seem a lifetime. Besides, he figured he already knew why she was dressed this way: there was going to be a full moon tonight, and she was just getting an early start.

"I bet you're wondering why I'm dressed like this," she said, in a squeaky voice.

Nolan said nothing, but he did manage a smile. Sort of.

"Normally I wouldn't be wearing this."

"Oh?"

"At least, not till tomorrow night. There's a convention going on, you know, comic books and 'Star Trek' and things, and the costume ball isn't till tomorrow night."

"Oh."

"This is just for the press conference. Some of us were asked to dress up now for the press conference. Some newspaper and TV people are here, doing interviews and stuff about the con. If you watch the six o'clock news, you just may see me."

The elevator was now at ballroom level, just a floor above the lobby. The doors slid open and, crowded in front of the ballroom entrance, were maybe a hundred and fifty people, mostly kids five years either side of Jon in age, some in strange get-ups, and cameramen and reporters and newsmen shuffling around, jockeying various equipment and holding mikes up to some people standing under klieg lights a shade brighter than the aurora borealis.

Nolan stepped to the rear of the elevator; he did not want to be on the six o'clock news.

The green girl shouted, "Scotty!" and ran out of the

elevator and into the crowd, toward a red-cheeked, roughly handsome dark-haired guy who looked familiar to Nolan; some television actor, he guessed. He caught the actor's eye and smiled sympathetically and the actor shook his head, as if to say, "I wish I was going down to the bar like you, my friend." The poor actor was swamped by girls and reporters, and Nolan wondered how anybody could ever stand going into a business as hair-raising as that.

The doors slid shut and Nolan got out at the lobby. He quickly went into the bar and had a Scotch, as much for that put-upon actor as himself.

Sitting on the stool next to him was a very pretty girl with short brown hair, wearing a chic pants outfit. Nolan gave her a look that asked if he could buy her one, and she gave him back a look that said he could.

"Gin and tonic," she said, in a voice designed to order gin and tonics.

Nolan glanced at his watch. He was running early. He hadn't really expected his buddy Bernie to be able to supply him with everything he needed, and so quickly. It was a good hour-and-a-half till he was supposed to meet Jon in the coffee shop, and he decided to kill some time.

He examined the girl's delicate but distinct features (her eyes were a hazel-green color you don't run into that often) and asked, "Model?"

She shook her head. "Flight attendant."

"Stewardess, you mean."

She gave him a firm little smile. "Flight attendant," she said.

"Don't worry."

"Don't worry what?"

"I don't believe what I read in paperbacks."

She laughed, and the bartender brought her the gin and

tonic. She looked at him, examining him in much the same way he had her. "Gangster?"

"Right the first time."

"Don't worry."

"Don't worry what?"

"I don't believe what I read in paperbacks, either."

They both laughed, and in her room on the tenth floor, forty-five minutes later, she kissed his cheek and played with the salt-and-pepper hair on his chest and said, "No, really, what are you?"

"I told you downstairs. Gangster, like you guessed."

"Come on."

"Very specialized gangster, though."

"Oh?"

"Yeah. All I do is see to it nobody gives Sinatra a bad time."

She laughed again, and the covers fell down around her waist, and he got a long look at her breasts. They were full, very, too full for her otherwise slender body, but he didn't mind. The nipples were small, which made the breasts look even bigger. They were coral color, her nipples, and he liked them. He leaned over and nibbled one.

"Hey!" she said. "You're a horny S.O.B., aren't you? Don't be a glutton."

"Lady," he said, between nibbles, "I'll take all the servings I can get. I don't often eat at restaurants this nice."

"Quit it," she giggled, in a tone that said go ahead.

Ahead was where he went, and they had a good time, their second. Nolan believed in going twice whenever possible, because the second time can be done slow and lovingly, without the urgency that makes the first round so good but so frantic. She had an ass as nice as her breasts, not skinny like the rest of her; something soft and fleshy and fun to fill his hands with.

She was doing him a lot of good: his bridges with Sherry were getting burned a bit faster than he had anticipated, and that was a relief. He realized his separation from Sherry had been a little heavy on his mind, and though he hated to admit it, even to himself, he missed the girl, damn it; and he didn't like going into a heist with that sort of emotional preoccupation working on him.

So sex this afternoon was a real lucky break for him. Made him feel purged. Made him feel great, like a fucking kid.

"Don't get the wrong idea," she said, sitting up again, her breasts hanging loose now, sagging just a little, as though tuckered out.

"Wrong idea about you?" he said. "Or about stewardesses?"

She grinned; a good grin, the sort many pretty girls avoid. "Either one. Want a smoke?"

"No. Gave 'em up."

"How come?"

"Not healthy. Man gets to be my age, he better watch his ass."

"What do you mean 'your age'? How old are you, anyway?"

"Forty-eight," Nolan lied.

"That's not so old. I'm thirty-five, which is kind of old for a flight attendant."

At least thirty-five, Nolan thought, saying, "You look like twenty, kid." He stroked a breast. Kissed her neck.

"Hey, give me a break . . . enough's enough. For right now, anyway. So tell me, what is your racket? What are you doing in Detroit?"

"I manage a nightclub, Chicago area," he said. (Which was semi-true, after all: the Tropical did use entertainment in their bar setup.) He told her that a friend of his, an old army buddy, had a little talent agency up here, and he'd promised to check out some of the guy's new clients.

"Oh really? You done that already?"

"No. Tonight. Going out to his place tonight and see what he has to offer."

"Sounds like fun. Care for some company?"

"Naw . . . it'll be a drag. This guy's agency is really small-time, I'm just looking at these acts out of friendship. Or pity. You'd fall asleep, the acts'll be so bad."

She made a face. "Well, looks like another rip-snorter of an evening for old coffee-tea-or-me," she said, apparently feeling brushed off. "Suppose I'll just catch another movie tonight, and if I'm lucky maybe get molested walking back to the hotel."

"Don't give me that," he said. "I can't picture you sitting home alone unless you wanted to."

"I thought you said you didn't believe what you read in paperbacks? My life isn't any swinging party. This is the first time I've gotten any in weeks."

"Bullshit."

"No, really. I been a lousy *nun* lately. Ever since my marriage broke up, last year."

"You were married? I thought a stewardess had to be single."

"Haven't you heard of Women's Lib and equal rights and all? The airlines can't pull much of that crap these days, though God knows they'd like to. And in my case, maybe I'd be better off, at least as far as the old anti-wedlock rule goes. The marriage, it just didn't work out, with my being a flight attendant and gone days at a time. My husband was balling some secretary at his office, some mousy little twerp with boobs like ping pong balls."

Nolan shrugged. "Then losing him should be no great loss. He's obviously an idiot. But there's plenty of other guys in the world."

"Yeah, and plenty of other idiots, too. Like there's this pilot who's been chasing me, but he's married, and he's obnoxious as hell too, so I been ducking him. I have had a fling or two, tiny ones, with some interesting passengers I've met on longer flights. But those guys also are married, usually, and I come out of an afternoon like this one feeling like a whore or something. How about you?"

"I never feel like a whore."

"I mean, are you married? Don't be a prick." She said "prick" in a nice way, with affection.

"Not married. Never have been. It's an institution that holds little appeal to me."

"After a two-year marriage that was just slightly less successful than the war in Vietnam, I tend to agree with you. Hey, you know something?"

"What?"

"I sort of like you. Your personality is a little on the sour side, but I like it. And your sexual enthusiasm, especially considering you think of yourself as an old man, has me somewhat winded, I'll admit, but I like that too. Let me make you a proposition. Why don't you come back tonight and see me, when you're through hearing those auditions? Then we can resume our conversation . . . and whatever else you'd care to resume."

"It could be late."

"I'll give you the spare key. Let yourself in and crawl under the covers with me. How does that sound to you?"

Nolan smiled. "That sounds fine."

They chatted for a while longer, and she mentioned that she had a flight tomorrow, and he mentioned he'd be taking a flight tomorrow himself, and it turned out to be the same one. That was a happy coincidence, and Nolan felt unnaturally pleased that this afternoon's encounter would be continued tonight and, in a way, on the plane tomorrow. In his younger days, he preferred light involvement with his women, in-and-out situations; but he found, as he grew older, that he liked-something more—not much more, maybe, but something.

He got dressed, and as he went to the door, he turned and said, "Hey! Your name. What the hell is it?"

"Hazel."

"Like your eyes," he said.

"Like the fat maid in the funnies," she said, squinching her nose.

"Well, you're in the right hotel for that"

"Yeah, I noticed. Comic book fans all over the place, kids in costumes, kids wearing T-shirts with cartoon characters on them. A kid with a T-shirt like that tried to pick me up in the bar, just before you showed, would you believe it?"

"Sure, woodwork's full of 'em. Listen, I got to get going. I'll see you tonight"

"Okay. Hey!"

"What?"

"Your name? What's your name?"

He hesitated for a moment; he better not use the Logan name. He was registered as Ryan, but for some reason he wanted to give her the name he himself felt most comfortable with. So he said, "Nolan," and to hell with it

"Is that a first name," she asked, "or a last?"

"Whatever you want," he said, and went out.

This time he had the elevator to himself, and damn glad of it.

Jon was in the coffee shop, working on a Coke.

Nolan joined him at the counter, said, "How much you blow on funny-books so far?"

The kid grinned. "Four hundred and thirty-five bucks and feeling no pain."

Nolan had no criticism of that. It was a harmless enough indulgence. Besides, he remembered Jon showing him a copy of a comic book, two years ago when he first met the kid; the comic had cost Jon two hundred bucks, which had seemed insane to Nolan, but just recently he had seen an article about an eighteen-year-old kid who'd paid eighteen hundred dollars for that same comic. Nolan asked Jon about it at the time, and Jon had said, rather bitterly, "That stupid clod . . . with him shelling out all that dough, and with all the news coverage he got, shit, prices'll inflate like crazy again. That comic wasn't worth any eighteen hundred bucks. Why, it wasn't worth a penny more than a grand."

Considering the interest Jon had made on his two-hundred-buck investment, Nolan was impressed, and no longer ridiculed his young friend's hobby. In fact, he counted himself a sucker, because he too had owned that comic book (bought it off the stands, when he was a kid) and after reading it had thrown his dime investment in the trash.

"How'd it go, Nolan?"

"We have wheels. No problem."

"Good. Rest of the stuff, too?"

"Rest of the stuff, too."

"What about the farmhouse?"

"Drove out there, had a look around. No, nobody saw me. I drew up a layout of the farm and all. We can go over it later, up in the room."

"Fine."

"Nervous?"

"Yes."

"Thought the funny-books would distract you."

"Me too. No soap. Tried to pick up a woman in the bar to see if *that* would distract me. But it fizzled too."

Nolan glanced at Jon's Wonder Warthog T-shirt, and wondered if—but no, that was ridiculous.

"Look, kid, there's one thing I want you to do for me."

"What's that?"

"Go buy some hose."

"Sure. Go buy some hose? Like rubber hose?"

"Like nylon hose. The kind women stick their legs in."

"Stockings? What the hell for, Nolan?"

"I thought we'd pose as Avon ladies."

"Oh. You mean masks. We'll pull 'em over our heads, you mean."

"Just buy them."

"Why didn't you?"

"I don't want to go in buying hose. What're you, crazy?"

"Too embarrassing?" Jon smiled.

"Hell yes. Why don't *you* want to?"

"Too embarrassing," Jon admitted.

"Right, and I'm in charge, you're my flunky, and when I say buy hose, goddammit, you buy hose."

"Well, they'll probably take me for some kind of pervert or something."

"Probably." Nolan grinned. He was in a good mood.

"What are you so happy about?"

"It's going to be clockwork, kid. We're going to fill our pockets with Sam Comfort's ill-gotten gains, and he won't be the wiser."

Now Jon was grinning too. "You make me feel better. I don't think I'm nervous, anymore. I don't even mind buying the hose. If the salesgirl asks me what I want nylons for, I'll just tell her I want 'em 'cause they'll go so good with my black lace garter belt."

"That's the spirit, kid. Here, I'll even pay for your damn Coke."

8

IT WAS FRIDAY evening, eight-fifteen. The country was calm and quiet tonight, the traffic along this gravel back road seemingly nonexistent. Across the way was a two-story gray frame farmhouse, beginning to sag, whose paint was peeling like an over-baked sunbather. It was a slovenly, ramshackle structure, a shack got out of hand; it sat in a big yard overgrown with big weeds, its location remote even for the country, the lights of neighboring farmhouses barely within view. The place was, in effect, isolated from civilization, which suited the people who lived there. And it suited Nolan and Jon's purpose, as well.

Jon had been studying the hovel the Comfort clan called home. He shook his head. "Dogpatch," he muttered.

"What?" Nolan said.

They were sitting in the dark blue, year-old Ford Nolan had leased from Bernie that afternoon. The motor was off, lights too; the car was parked in a cornfield across the road from the Comfort homestead. They were a good half-block down from the house, the nose of the car approaching but not edging onto the dirt access inlet that bridged ditch and gravel road. They had entered a similar access inlet to cross the corner of the field, having cut their lights as they drove down the road that eventually would have intersected the one running past the Comfort house. They'd rumbled slowly across the recently harvested ground, like some prehistoric beast lumbering after its prey at snail's pace. The only sound had been that of corn husks cracking under the wheels, but the stillness of the night and the insecurity of the situation had magnified that husk-cracking in Jon's perception, unsettling him. The moon seemed to Jon a huge searchlight illuminating the field, making him feel naked, exposed, unsettling him further. But nothing had happened, and now they sat in the car, in the cornfield, getting ready. They were dressed for their work, in black: Nolan in knit slacks and turtleneck sweater; Jon in jeans and sweatshirt (the latter worn inside-out because the other side bore a fluorescent Batman insignia). The clothes were heavy, warm, which was good, as the night was a cool, almost cold one. Both wore guns in holsters on their hips, police-style: .38 Colt revolvers with four-inch barrels, butts facing out. Between them on the seat were two olive-drab canisters, looking much like beer cans, but with military markings in place of brand names, and levers connecting to pin mechanisms. Also on the seat was a package of nylon stockings, unopened.

Jon let his Dogpatch remark lie; he'd just been thinking aloud, and though Nolan had been very tolerant lately about Jon's comics hobby, now was no time to put that tolerance to a test by going into the resemblance the Comfort place held to something Al Capp might have drawn.

Nolan said, "You want me to go over it once more?"

"No," Jon said.

"Okay." Nolan was sitting back in the seat, loose, apparently relaxed, but Jon thought he sensed an uncharacteristic tightness in the man's voice, perhaps brought on by concern over Jon's relative inexperience in matters of potential violence.

They'd been over the plan several times, first at the hotel, in their room, and again on the way here, in the car. Nolan would come up behind the Com¬fort farmhouse, through the pasture in back; the ground was open, open as hell, but there were trees along the property line, and also a barn, and those would provide whatever cover Nolan needed. Jon would allow Nolan five minutes, during which time Nolan would jimmy the basement window open, crawl inside, deposit his calling card, and crawl out After those five minutes were up, Jon would initiate phase two of the plan, in that weed-encroached front yard.

Jon felt sure everything would go without a hitch, but he wished he could also be sure Nolan felt the same way. Jon's own confidence was undercut somewhat by the lack of confidence he suspected in Nolan, an attitude that stemmed back to that discussion they'd had about firearms, back at the hotel.

"I don't exactly understand," Jon had said, "how we're going to subdue these dudes—I mean, what do we do, brain 'em with the butts of our guns, or what?"

"For Chrissake, kid," Nolan had answered, eyes narrowed even more than usual, "never go swinging a gun butt around. You got the barrel pointing at you, and you can end up with a hole in your chest big as the one in your damn head. Why do you think I prefer a long-barreled gun?"

"Better aim, you said."

"Yeah, that. And this too—with a long barreled gun you can put a guy to sleep without firing a shot."

"So, what then? We brain 'em with the gun barrels?"

"You would if it was called for. But it isn't. I told you what the plan was, and you didn't hear any part where you go slugging people with a gun, did you? All right, then.

You just leave the subduing to me—and leave the gun in its holster, dig?"

"Look, I'm capable of using it if I have to, Nolan."

"Maybe, but don't act like it's something to look forward to. By now, you been through enough shit like this to tell the difference between what we're about to do and some goddamn comic-book fairy tale. If we get in a totally desperate situation, sure, use the gun. That's what it's there for. But since we got the element of surprise working for us, I don't see that happening."

Jon was determined now to make a good showing tonight, to regain Nolan's confidence by behaving like a cold, hard-ass professional, not like some naive kid. Next to him, Nolan was opening the package of nylons, and Jon listened to the crackle of cellophane and waited for Nolan to hand him one of the stockings.

But instead there was a long moment of silence, and even in darkness Jon had no trouble making out the stunned look on Nolan's face.

"Kid."

"Yeah?"

"I think we're going to have to make a change of plan."

"Oh?"

"Yeah. I don't think we're going to be able to split up. You're going to have to follow along pretty close behind me."

"Why's that?"

Nolan held up the nylons.

Panty hose.

"Panty hose," Nolan said.

Jon started to sputter. "Nolan, shit, I mean, that's all the girls are wearing these days. I should've checked to make sure they were the old-fashioned kind. I mean . . ."

Nolan dug in his pocket and got out his knife.

"Nolan—what're you doing?"

A grin flashed under Nolan's mustache, a grin so wide and out of character, it startled Jon. "I'm not going to kill you, kid," he said, "I just got to perform some hasty surgery."

Nolan separated the siamese twins; he handed one amputated leg to Jon and kept the other. "You know, kid," Nolan said, "this is a hell of a lot of trouble to go to, just to get your way."

"Get my way?"

"Yeah. But you win. From now on, I buy all the nylons."

They both grinned this time, and enthusiasm ran through Jon like a drug. "I won't let you down, Nolan."

"I know you won't."

Nolan pulled the stocking over his head, immediately disfiguring himself. "Five minutes, Jon."

"Five minutes, Nolan."

And Nolan was gone.

Five minutes? Five hours was what it seemed. Jon made a concerted effort not to study his watch, not to follow the second hand around. But he did, of course, and the time was excruciatingly slow in passing, the seconds pelting him like the liquid pellets of the Chinese water torture; the ticking of his watch seemed abnormally loud, as if in an echo chamber, and he wondered how the hell a relic like that (a Dick Tracy watch, circa late '30s) could put out such a racket.

He thought he saw something moving across the road, over in the Comfort yard, but it was only the tall weeds getting pushed around by the wind. That brought his attention to the farmhouse, which was what he was supposed to be doing anyway—watching the house, keeping alert for anything out of order that might be going on over there. The Comforts couldn't be expected to stick to Nolan and Jon's game plan, after all; and as Nolan had said more than once, you never can tell when the human element might enter in and knock a well-conceived plan on its well-conceived ass.

Jon sat studying the old gray two-story, and thought back to the verbal tour of the place Breen had given him last night. Though from the run-down exterior you'd never guess it, the Comfort castle was, according to Breen, expensively furnished and equipped with modern appliances and gadgetry galore. Its shabby appearance was no doubt partially purposeful at least; as a thief himself, old Sam Comfort would have an unnaturally suspicious and devious mind, certainly capable of devising a defense of this sort: that is, living in a house that looked like a junk heap on the outside, but was a palace on the inside. Crafty as hell, because judging from what he could see, Jon could hardly imagine a less likely prospect for a robbery. Looting a place like that—why, you'd be lucky to come away with a six-pack of beer and a handful of food stamps.

Not that they had in mind stealing any of the possessions the Comforts had acquired through years of applied larceny; the creature comforts the Comfort creatures had assembled for themselves were of no interest to Jon and Nolan. There was only one thing in that house that interested them: the strongbox of cash kept somewhere within those deceptively decayed walls. Breen had reported that old Sam kept a minimum of fifty thousand in that box at all times, and there was a good chance the Comforts (having just returned from Iowa City) hadn't yet banked their latest parking meter bonanza. Which meant, in all probability, that some two hundred grand was locked up within that metal box.

He checked his watch.

Thirty seconds shy of five minutes.

He withdrew the gun from the holster, hefted it, put it back. Took a deep breath. Another. The butterflies in his stomach began to disperse.

Ten seconds.

He pulled the nylon mask down over his face. It didn't impair his vision particularly, though he could feel it contorting his features, feel it tight on his face. It was a strange feeling, like pressing your face against a window.

Five minutes, and he left the Ford, got down in the ditch, and walked till he was across from the house, then crawled across the gravel road, moved up and over the opposite ditch, and into the high weeds of the Comforts' front yard. The weeds were more than sufficient cover; he traveled on his hands and knees and couldn't be seen. He was within a few yards of the house when he heard a muffled pop, and after a moment smoke began to fill the air. Nolan had said the smoke would penetrate, and penetrate it did, in spades. The smoke was curling out through openings the house didn't know it had, from around windows and between paint-peeling boards and from every damn where—gray, creeping smoke—and if Jon didn't know better, he'd have sworn the house was on fire.

Which was, of course, the idea.

To convince the Comforts their house was burning.

To panic the old man into grabbing his treasure box of loot and abandoning his ship.

By this time, Jon was right up by the cement steps that rose to the front door, and he pulled the pin on his little olive-drab can, which made it pop and sprayed out smoke, blowtorch fashion, to the accompaniment of a loud hissing sound. As he retreated to the tall weeds, Jon wondered how so much smoke could fit into one little can. Earlier, he'd asked Nolan about the canisters; why, he'd wanted to know, was the top of the can gray and the rest green? Because, Nolan explained, the green was for camouflage purposes, while the top of the can was marked the color of smoke it made. Jon almost wished they'd used one green smoke bomb and one red one; it wouldn't have looked like a fire, but it sure would've freaked out that pothead Billy Comfort. The poor burned-out bastard would've thought he was hallucinating.

Nolan should be coming around the house any time now. The smoke was thickening, but Jon wasn't having too much trouble maintaining a reasonable level of vision, even with the nylon mask. A figure was coming around from the left of the house. Must be Nolan, Jon thought, but then he saw the outline of the figure's head: it was a head with a bushy mane of hair, Afro-bushy.

It was Billy Comfort, speak of the goddamn devil.

The shaggy-haired figure was moving toward Jon, and Jon ducked behind the cement steps. Billy was carrying a pole of some sort, and though he apparently hadn't spotted Jon, he was heading straight for the smoke grenade, which was still spewing its gray guts out, hissing away like a big sick snake. As Billy approached, Jon suppressed a cough, covering his already nylon-covered mouth, wondering where the hell Nolan was, or, for that matter, old man Comfort.

Billy knelt beside the smoke grenade, fanning the fumes away with his free hand. He nudged the blisteringly hot canister with one foot, like a Neanderthal trying to figure out what fire was. Finally, he said, "Far fuckin' out," and began to laugh and cough simultaneously.

Jon's hand touched the butt of the .38 lightly. Nolan had

said leave the subduing to me, but Nolan wasn't around. Somebody had to subdue Billy Com-fort, and right now, before Billy went screaming out the truth of the deception to his old man.

So Jon did what he thought best.

He tackled Billy, burying his head in Billy's balls.

Billy yelped accordingly, and his foot connected with the smoking can and he slipped on it, like a contestant taking a fall in a log-rolling contest, and he went down hard, the air escaping from him in a big whoosh. Jon clasped a hand over Billy's mouth and grinned in what proved to be a premature victory, because Billy managed to swing something around that caught Jon on the side of the head and blacked him out.

When Jon awoke, seconds later, he saw right away what it was that had put him to sleep: the handle of that pole Billy was carrying, only it was more than just a pole: it was the wooden shaft of a five-pronged pitchfork. And Jon looked up through the smoke-and-nylon haze and saw in Billy's eyes a haze of another sort: a druggy haze. Billy was high, and Billy was on to the game. Maybe he'd even witnessed Jon and/or Nolan planting the smoke bombs; perhaps he'd been back in that barn, smoking or snorting or doing God-knows-what sort of dope, when he'd spied suspicious things going on up by the house, and had grabbed a pitchfork as a make-do weapon and come rushing to the rescue of home and hearth.

So that's how it stood: Billy with one foot on Jon's chest, smoke floating around them like a choking fog, Billy raising the pitchfork to impale Jon and put him to sleep again.

Permanently.

9

NOLAN CROSSED the gravel road in a crouch, hopped down into the ditch. It must have rained here recently, as the ditch was damp and got his shoes muddy. When he was safely within the sheltering trees that divided the Comfort land from the neighboring spread, Nolan cleaned his shoes off on the trunk of one of the clustered evergreens.

He was uncomfortable in the nylon mask; the thing was hot, even on a cool night like this. He pulled it off and stuffed it in his pants pocket. He'd put it back on when he got up by the house. Right now, he preferred having his vision completely unimpaired; enjoyed having the clear, crisp country air fill his lungs without a damn nylon filter.

Panty hose, he thought, and grinned momentarily.

In his left hand was the olive-drab canister, the U.S. Army smoke grenade identical to the one he'd left with Jon. With his right hand he withdrew the long-barreled .38 from the police holster; it was going to be necessary to rap a head or two, and perhaps do more than that, should something go out of kilter, despite what he'd told Jon about going easy with the firearms. He'd taught him well, but Jon's experience under fire was more than limited; if push came to shove, Jon would be armed, would be able to respond, but Nolan didn't want that kid waving a .38 around frivolously.

He stayed within the thick evergreens, got up parallel to the big gray barn and, crouching again, crossed half a block's worth of pasture and then flattened himself against the barn's back side. He could hear cattle or something stirring around in there, but not a Comfort, surely; the Comforts owned this land, according to Breen, but leased both pasture and barn to a farmer whose own property adjoined the Comforts' in back. Which made the Comforts a part of the landed gentry, Nolan supposed, which was a hell of a thought.

The house was maybe a hundred yards from the barn, maybe a shade more than that. Open ground and, with the moon full and the house fairly well lit up, not easily crossed unseen. He got on his hands and knees and began to crawl, like a commando training under the machine-gun fire of some square-jaw sergeant.

He crawled two feet, and his hand—the one with the gun in it—sank into something soft which, on closer examination, proved to be cow dung. Nolan wasn't happy about have gunk all over his hand, or his gun either, and wiped both clean on the grass. Holstering the .38, he swore to himself and crawled on. But the pasture was a cow-pattie minefield and, several feet later, the same hand ran into the same substance, a bit drier this time but no less irritating. So he said a mental "Fuck it," got back up in a crouch, and moved on. What the hell, he thought, it wasn't like the Comforts were out watching for him, and you can't expect a city boy to go crawling through cow shit, not for anybody or anything.

A barbed-wire fence separated the Comforts' yard from the pasture, and Nolan squeezed under the fence without so much as snagging his sweater—a much more successful enterprise than his aborted attempt at crawling across the cow-pattie beachhead. The weeds were waist high in the yard and, keeping in his low crouch, he proceeded until the weeds ended and the gravel drive, which circled the place, took over. The family Buick was parked alongside the house on the left, which meant it would be a toss-up which door Sam would head for—front or back—when the "fire" broke out. Before he left the high weeds to cross the drive,

Nolan got out the nylon mask, pulled it on, and drew the .38 again. Down to business, cow shit or no cow shit.

The house had many windows, and lights were on in most of the rooms, but all the window shades were drawn. This was frustrating, because Nolan had to make sure both father and son were present in the house, and where. The shade of one window on the right side of the house allowed an inch or two clearance at the bottom to peer through, and since Breen had given him a full layout of the house, it didn't surprise Nolan to find that the room beyond the window was the living room. He was, however, slightly surprised to find that Breen's description of the Comfort place had not been an exaggeration: the house really was as lavishly—and tastelessly—furnished as Breen had said. The living room had wall-to-wall red shag carpeting and a sofa and reclining chair covered in a yellowish leather; there were any number of heavy, expensive wood pieces of various and totally nonmatching styles, as well as a couple of clear plastic scoop-seated chairs. Everything in the room was of high quality, but was slapped together like a furniture store's warehouse sale. Drab, old, pale wallpaper, faded and peeling, was a backdrop to all this expensive but oddly coupled furniture, and the high point of the room was the Hamms beer sign over the sofa, lit from within, displaying a shifting panorama of shimmering "sky blue waters." Lying on the sofa, sipping a Hamms, basking in the glow of a color television console the size of a foreign car, was Sam Comfort—a skinny old man with a potbelly, wearing gray longjohns, the buttons open halfway down his chest He was watching "Hee-Haw."

None of the other, shaded windows around the house afforded Nolan any view, though from Breen's description he knew where everything was: adjacent to the living room was a kitchen (with space-age refrigerator, of course—stick a glass in a hole in the door and you get ice water) and Sam's bedroom, which were side by side and together took up the same space as the rather large living room; in there somewhere was a toilet—Nolan didn't remember exactly where—unless the Comforts still went the outhouse route, or maybe the cows weren't the only ones crapping in the pasture. According to Breen, the old man's room was unlike the others in the house, as it alone did not show signs of acquired affluence; the master bedroom was as empty and functional as the old man's mind. Upstairs was a bedroom for Terry (the statutory rapist presently being rehabilitated) and another for Billy—also an office affair Sam used for planning sessions and the like. Nolan could see colored lights flashing behind the shade on Billy's window; Breen said Billy's room was a pot freak's retreat, water bed and strobe lights and black-light posters and tons of stereo equipment, enough wattage in the latter to power a fair-size radio station. He could hear the faint throb of rock music coming from that upper floor room, and he would have to make the hopefully safe assumption that Billy was mind-tripping up there, as was the boy's usual practice.

Satisfied that he'd pinpointed both Comforts, Nolan went to work on the basement window in back of the house. The window came open easily, soundlessly, with the proper prying from his knife. He climbed down inside the Comforts' lowest level, a washing machine right below the window serving as a step down for him, making his entry a quiet one.

He used a pen-flash to examine the room. This end of the long basement was the laundry room; the other was being converted into a bar and recreation area. This was the first remodeling the Comforts had undertaken, and they were apparently doing the work themselves, as it was pretty slipshod: boards, cans of paint, various building bullshit lying around.

Which was good, because this was the makings of a fire hazard; this made a logical reason for a basement fire, and should help to con Sam as he quickly tried to make some logic out of a fire breaking out in his house. The remodeling was almost finished, but not quite: the bar was in and linoleum was on the floor, but the ceiling wasn't tiled, which was also good: those open ceiling beams would insure the effectiveness of the smoke bomb's penetration.

Nolan knelt with the canister, pulled the lever, heard its *pop*, left it on the floor, mid-basement, turning his head away even before he'd let go of the can, as already its stream of smoke was shooting out like water from a firehose. The can hissed as it dispersed its contents, and Nolan headed toward the laundry end of the basement, then hopped up onto the washing machine and out the window.

He immediately returned to his view of Sam Comfort relaxing in the living room. A smile formed under the nylon mask as Nolan watched bewilderment grow on Sam's face, first as Sam sniffed smoke, then as he *saw* smoke. After a slapstick double-take, the old clown jumped from the couch as if goosed and ran upstairs via the stairwell opening in the far corner of the room. The positioning of those stairs was a break for Nolan; with this view of the action, he'd be able to key on whether or not Sam opted for the front door, here in the living room, or the back door, out in the kitchen. Sam was only gone half a minute, then came tumbling out of the stairwell, a man who'd all but fallen down the stairs, coughing from the ever-thickening smoke, showing signs of panic, shaking in his damn underwear. As Sam came into clearer view in that smoke-clogged receptacle of a room, Nolan could see plainly under one of Sam's arms an oversize green metal strongbox—*Bingo!*— while slung over Sam's other arm was a double-barreled shotgun. He's panicked all right, Nolan thought, but the old coot's as suspicious and crafty as ever.

A sound—*pop!*—turned Nolan's head, in reflex, before he realized the sound was only Jon's smoke grenade going off, meaning things were running to plan. When he turned back, the old man was no longer in sight.

Shit! The room was pretty well dense with smoke now, and Nolan couldn't tell if the front door was slightly ajar, which would have indicated whether Sam had gone out that way. Damn it, there was nothing to do but circle behind the house, and if Sam wasn't back there, come on around and catch him out the front. Damn!

Nolan ran.

Sam wasn't in back, nor was the back door ajar.

Alongside the house, where the Buick was, no sign of Sam there, either.

And what about Billy? An ugly chain of deduction was forming in Nolan's mind. Sam had gone upstairs for three reasons, hadn't he? To get the strongbox; to grab the shotgun; to warn his boy Billy. But Sam hadn't been up there very long, barely long enough to do all those things. Why hadn't Billy been following along on his daddy's heels, down those steps? Why hadn't Sam yelled "Fire!" when smoke first began trailing into the room, to warn Billy immediately? Shouldn't that have been Sam's natural reaction?

If, then, Billy hadn't been upstairs, where had he been? And more important, where the hell was he now?

Once around the front of the house, Nolan knew the

answer to that. Nolan's questions about Billy were, for the most part, anyway, answered: Billy had not been in the house; Billy had been outside, Christ knows why or where. And Billy was onto the "burning house" trick. In fact, Billy was right next to the smoke grenade Jon had planted.

And Billy was grinning. The smoke was just as thick out here as in the house, but Nolan could see that Billy was grinning. Billy was laughing, or was doing something like laughing, a combination of rasping smoke-cough and sick snickering. Billy was stoned out of his head, and Billy was standing with one foot on Jon's chest, getting ready to heave one mother of a pitchfork down into Jon, punching steel teeth through the kid, pinning him to the earth like a scarecrow.

Nolan was still running, a slow but steady jog, and he bumped into Sam, who'd come out the front door, and the two men came face to face and for just a moment. Nylon mask or no, Nolan felt he could sense recognition in Sam's flat gray eyes.

Nolan slapped the old man across the side of the face with the .38 and Sam said, "Unggh!" and toppled, colliding with Nolan. Nolan hit the ground and was on his feet again within the same second, and he brought up the .38 and fired twice.

The shots broke the country calm like cracks of thunder. The bullets hit Billy Comfort in the chest and rocked him, shook him like a naughty child, exploded through him, blood squirting from the front of him, a spatter of bone and organs and more blood bursting out his back. He pitched backward, gurgling, dying.

Jon was awake now and rolling to one side as Billy Comfort's last effort in life—the hurling of the pitchfork—came to no account: the fork quivered in the ground, right next to Jon, but not, thankfully, in him.

Nolan looked at Jon and, with their stocking-distorted features, they exchanged a look that had in it any number of things—relief and shock and frustration among them, perhaps regret as well—and suddenly Jon's face distorted further under the mask, as he yelled, "Nolan! The old man!"

And as he remembered Sam Comfort, whom he'd merely cuffed out of the way so he could take care of more important business, as he recalled the crazy old man with a shotgun, Nolan heard the country calm shatter a second time in gunfire.

Interim: Takeoff

10

CAROL SAID, *"I WISH* I was going with you."

Ken made a face at her in the bedroom mirror, as if to say, *Don't be ridiculous,* and went on strapping the emergency parachute to his stomach, over his black cotton pullover. On the bed, closed, locked, was the suitcase with the fake bomb in it. The suitcase was a cheap, tan overnight bag they'd picked up at a discount department store. "Picked up" was literally right: Ken had shoplifted the suitcase, much to Carol's discomfort, and the thought of that afternoon, several weeks ago, still gave her something of a chill.

Ken had said he didn't want to leave anything behind that could be traced to him, and he felt purchasing any such items locally would be dangerous. Carol didn't agree: the items he had in mind (the suitcase, some clothes, a wig) could be purchased at any large chain store and should be virtually untraceable. How could you tell, for example, which of the hundreds of thousands of stores an overnight bag had been purchased from?

But Ken had poured out a stream of double-talk, saying many items were code-marked for certain distribution areas, and skyjacking was a federal offense of the most serious nature, and those FBI men can trace a piece of string to the shirt on your back and blah blah blah. Carol didn't believe any of it, but realized that Ken probably didn't either. There was some secret reason he hadn't divulged to her yet for his going one hundred miles to a discount department store to purchase the items at all: he was going to shoplift them—a bit of news he saved for Carol until they were parked in the discount store's huge parking lot.

"You will cover for me," he said. "Make sure none of the floor-walkers or sales people see me."

"But Ken . . . this is crazy."

She looked across the sea of cars—it was Saturday, and the only parking space they'd found was at the rear of the endless lot—and even from this distance the store looked gigantic, some grotesque national monument to commercialism. Though the massive building was a pinkish brick, its face was primarily steel-trimmed glass, topped with enormous neon letters that said BARGAIN CITY. She knew, without ever having been in there, that those rows and rows of doors would open onto an entryway big enough to put their house in, an entryway lined with bubble gum machines and armed guards.

Wasn't Saturday the worst possible day to go shoplifting? All those people? All those people were precisely why Saturday was ideal, Ken said; there'd be too many people for store personnel to keep track of. Carol didn't quite buy that line of reasoning, either, but she went along with Ken. When push came to shove, she always went along with Ken.

She realized it wasn't stylish these days to let your husband—or any man—control your life. But she wasn't a liberated woman, and had no desire to be one. That point of view came from being the last of six children, she supposed, all the rest of whom were boys. She'd been the little sis, and she and her mother had lived in the shadow of her father and his five sons. And it hadn't been so bad. Being the only sister of five brothers had plenty of advantages, and she was the baby of the family besides and accordingly was awarded extra attention: on a holiday, she'd get more gifts, more kisses, than anyone.

Still, a big part of her childhood had been learning to keep her place. As the youngest child, you learned that anyway, and as the youngest and a girl, you got used to having your life controlled for you; your decisions made for you; your thinking done for you. You got used to having men dominate your world.

Ken had been just the kind of man she was used to. They'd met at a junior college in their hometown, in downstate Missouri, and he had been the firm but gentle sort of guy she'd been looking for, always. It hadn't been hard to grab him; she was aware of her good looks, and Ken was a loner whose nonconformist ways had turned off most of the girls he'd dated—he'd rather spend Friday night working on some electronics project than at a movie, say, or a dance. He had a quiet strength she liked, and he was cute, and while he wasn't thoughtful, he certainly wasn't cruel. Besides, she was used to having self-centered men around her. Wasn't that the way of all men? The ones worth having, anyway.

There was a side to Ken that bothered her, when she got to know him better; but she'd cherished the flaw in him, rather than rejected him because of it. By the time she noticed his weak spot, she was already hopelessly in love with him, so her reaction was positive: the flaw in Ken was something she could, in her quiet way, help him with; she could give him the encouragement to overcome his one weakness.

His weakness was that he had a tendency not to finish things. He had a fine mind, brilliant, really; he could do most anything. But his mind moved so quickly, his enthusiasm shifted so rapidly, that he often did not complete what he'd started. He'd flunked out of the junior college, primarily because he had no interest in the subjects he was taking, and one just doesn't flunk out of J.C.—J.C. is where a person goes 'cause he might flunk out (or already *had*) someplace else.

After they were married, Ken had gone to Greystoke Teacher's College, while Carol worked as a secretary and helped put him through, and he finally graduated after an extra semester. Greystoke was an expensive school that ate up much of what Ken's parents had left him, not to mention most of Carol's weekly paycheck; but Greystoke was a special sort of college, a school for students who hadn't hacked it elsewhere, an educational court of last resort, guaranteed to graduate its enrollees. Mostly rich kids from back east made use of Greystoke, just so they could pick up a token degree. Some years it was accredited, others it was not. Fortunately for Ken, his was one of the accredited years, though with the school's poor reputation, it hardly mattered. Not that the odds of landing a good job with a

Greystoke degree were bad; why, they were excellent—
provided you were the son of some tycoon.

So she'd watched, reluctantly, while Ken took the
salesman job, selling Florida real estate with a pitch that
included a free meal and the showing of a film. Ken would
go into towns of medium size, mostly, with the dinner
invitations already sent out, and proceed with his routine.
He didn't know where the company got its mailing lists,
but the prospects who attended the dinners were excellent,
couples nearing retirement who were ripe for a good land
offer. It was a lucrative field, though Carol was bothered by
the fact that the company sales pitch sounded
uncomfortably like a con game. Ken assured her it was on
the up and up. And she'd finally been convinced, because
after all, hadn't the sales executive invited them to Florida
to give Ken a first-hand look at the land he was selling?
And they'd gone, they'd seen it; it was gorgeous land;
they'd bought a chunk of it themselves.

Of course, that had been part of the deal: Ken had to
invest in a lot of his own and become a stockholder,
purchasing a specified minimum number of shares. That
had taken the last of the money his parents had left him—
just over ten thousand dollars. But what better investment
was there than land?

This time Ken hadn't been a quitter, and Carol had been
so proud of him. For three years he sold the lots, and he and
Carol racked up quite a savings—as one of the company's
top salesmen, Ken was regularly offered stock options, and
they fed over half of Ken's earnings into Dream-Land. And
they'd bought the house in Canker with a bank loan,
choosing the quiet little town so they could be close enough
to Carol's family to make visiting easy, but far enough
away to enjoy privacy. Ken's plan was to keep selling for

another three years, and then they'd have amassed enough stock for him to borrow against and open up a small TV and radio repair shop, which would be ideal for him and for Carol, too, who didn't like sharing her husband with the road.

Ken's investment of his time and money had assured Carol that her husband's flaw—that tendency not to finish what he started, which came from a certain immaturity—was now a thing of the past, a wound healed over, with not even a sign of scar tissue.

But wounds can open up after the longest time, if enough pressure is applied to them. And pressure in this instance emerged in the form of Ken's aptly named parent company, Florida Dream-Land Realtors.

Part of Ken's pitch had included pointing out that, while the cash outlay for a piece of Dream-Land land was amazingly low, that low price was made possible by holding off actual development of the land, actual building of homes, until 70 percent of the lots had been sold. Of course, a buyer couldn't be expected to wait forever for his home and his land, so a projected date (five years hence, from Dream-Land's first sale) was set for development to begin. This was guaranteed; either said development began, or the buyer's money would be returned, with the buyer retaining full ownership of his lot.

All of which sounded swell, both to salesmen like Ken and to prospective buyers, most of whom were far enough away from retirement that waiting a few years for their dream land was no problem. Five years wasn't so long.

But long enough for a swindle.

Plenty long enough for that. Oh, the land was down there, all right; everybody who bought a lot owned a slice of Florida land. But not the land in the film Ken had shown to the people at the invitation-only dinners; not the land the sales exec had pointed out to Ken and Carol on their trip down there. The land in the film, the land the exec pointed out, belonged to somebody else.

Dream-Land was Florida land, too.

Swampland.

Uninhabitable damn swampland that could gag an alligator; dream land that was a nightmare. And Ken and all the other salesmen and the folks they'd sold the land to, all of them, were stuck in that swamp up to their rears.

The only happy aspect was that Ken himself, and most of the other salesmen, were in no way liable for the fraud perpetrated; they, like everybody in it (except the Dream-Land wheels) were the butt of the joke.

So there they sat, in Canker, Missouri, with over three years of their lives wasted, no savings, not a damn thing — except a mortgaged house and plans that had fizzled into nothing.

But you can always make new plans, and Ken came up with one. Carol hadn't liked it from the outset, but what could she say? Ken was, after all, the man of the house.

But sometimes bowing to every wish of the "man of the house" could go too far. She shouldn't be expected to do something she would hate herself for doing. Like helping him on this crazy skyjacking thing. Even aiding and abetting his silly, stupid shoplifting. There just wasn't any sane *reason* for it; no logic to it. And besides, she didn't for the life of her see how he was going to get the shoplifting done. He had picked the suitcase up first, actually just tucked it under his arm, then strolled around the store, and while she kept an eye peeled, he'd slipped the various items in: curly brown wig, some sunglasses, green corduroy shirt, and some jeans.

"How are you going to get past the registers?" she asked him.

"Just watch," he said, and headed to the front of the store. There was a coffee shop up on the right, off to one side of the rows of check-out counters. They sat in a booth in the shop, and Ken carefully drew a folded-up sack from his pocket, a large sack with the discount store's name on it. He put the suitcase inside. When that was done, she followed as he slid past the check-out counters, mixing in with the shoppers pouring out of them, and with the suitcase-in-sack snugly under his arm, went out the door.

Past several armed guards who were standing by that door for the express purpose of nabbing shop-lifters. No one questioned him. Nothing.

In the car, she found she was panting. Sweat was rolling down her cheeks, though the day was a cool, overcast one. "What would you have done," she managed to ask, "if someone stopped you?"

"I was prepared for that," he said, the tone of his voice implying he'd almost been hoping for that, as well. "I had a story ready."

"What kind of story?"

'That I'd seen a lady drop this package in the coffee shop and was going out into the lot after her, to give her her package."

"But there would be no sales slip in the sack."

"So what? It was her package, not mine."

"Do you think they would have believed you, Ken? Do you honestly think they would've believed you?"

"Been interesting to find out, wouldn't it?"

They drove fifty miles and then Ken stopped for lunch, but Carol didn't order anything. Her stomach was still jumping. All the while, sitting in the car, she'd been expecting a highway patrol car to come screaming up behind them. The heavyset Broderick Crawford cop would say, "Okay kids, let's have a look at that suitcase there in the back seat." He had never shown up, of course, but he was there in her mind, the cop and his car and siren and gun.

Finally, she consented to a grilled cheese sandwich, which she nibbled at. She said, "I never stole anything before, Ken."

And Ken looked at her, and there was something in his eyes, a damn twinkling in his eyes. He grinned and said, "Me neither."

There it was: the reason. The secret purpose of the trip. The skyjacking he'd been planning, this new, obscenely dangerous project, this terrifyingly large-scale *crime* he was going to commit, was the first time he'd ever even contemplated breaking the rules.

Ken. Conservative Ken. Arrow-straight Ken. It was quite a leap from shoplifter to skyjacker, but an even bigger one from Eagle Scout to skyjacker. She understood that now.

She understood that in a crazy way the shoplifting had been a trial run, as well as an absurd ritual of self-initiation; that had Ken been caught and been unable to bluff his way out of the situation, he would have taken it as, well a *sign*, an indication from somewhere that he was in way over his head. That this should be another project left unfinished.

But he hadn't been caught, and here they were, weeks later, the skyjack plan finally going into effect.

Ken seemed very calm, the late afternoon sunlight filtering through the filmy pink curtains of the bedroom window and bathing him in a golden, contented glow; he seemed almost peaceful, as he neatly assembled himself, climbing into the green shirt, which fit over the chute as though he had a paunch. It was as if he was assembling the components of one of his electronics gadgets. *Could he really be so cool?* Carol wondered. *Did that silly afternoon of shoplifting free him so from worry?*

She wouldn't be free from worry, not until she had him back again, in their house, in this bed. Her only consolation was that the bomb in the stolen suitcase was a dummy. Carol wondered for a moment why Ken would have spent so much time building a mock bomb into the suitcase. This, like his shoplifting escapade, was almost eccentric aspect to the "project" that Carol would never completely understand. She just took comfort in knowing that her Ken could never really hurt anybody, let alone blow up a planeload of people.

She touched his shoulder, caught his eyes in the mirror, and held them. "Maybe something will happen. Something you haven't thought of. Maybe . . . maybe we won't ever see each other again."

This time he *really* made a face. This time he said it out loud: "Don't be ridiculous."

And he looked away.

Fifteen minutes later, they were in the car, and she was driving him the eight miles to a town where no one knew them, where he could catch the bus to Detroit. She felt uncomfortable in the driver's seat

Three

11

LIKE ALL AIRPORT restaurants, this one was lousy. The $2 hamburger was cold, the potato chips stale, the Coke flat and mostly ice. Jon looked out the window. The sky was overcast. Right in front of him, some men in coveralls were stuffing the belly of a 727 with luggage; behind them stretched an endless concrete sea of runway, planes taxiing around as if wandering aimlessly. It was a gray day. Jon's was a gray mood.

The Detroit airport was a cold, monolithic assemblage that didn't exactly cheer Jon up, its overall design a vaguely modernistic absence of personality, heavy on dreary, neutral-color stone, and its infinite intersecting halls converging on a toweringly high-ceilinged lobby in what might have been intended as a tribute to confusion. The only thing he liked about the place was that, compared to Chicago's O'Hare, there were fewer people and, consequently, not as much frantic rushing around. But the less hectic pace didn't do Jon any good, really; it only gave him time to reflect on things that were better left alone. It gave him time for a gray mood.

And he was tired. He'd been up all night practically, watching movies—not on the tube, but in a ballroom at the hotel, with hundreds of other voluntary insomniacs. The showing of old films ("from eight till dawn") was a traditional part of a comic book convention, and when he got back to the hotel after the Comfort bloodbath, he figured he might as well enjoy himself, he wouldn't be getting much sleep that night, anyway. Not after what happened.

He'd made a point of not sitting with anyone he knew and, despite the common interests he shared with those around him, avoided conversation, and struck up no new acquaintances among his fellow fans. His hope was that he'd lose himself in the flickering fantasy up on the screen, and so he sat watching, all but numb, leaning back in the uncomfortable steel folding chair and letting the Marx Brothers and Buster Crabbe as Flash Gordon and any number of monster movies roll over him in a celluloid tide. Jon and the rest of the crowd followed the films through most of the night; the feature set for a 4:30 A.M. screening was worth staying for: the original 1933 *King Kong*, and Jon thought to himself, *This is where I came in.*

After that, the crowd had thinned, even the diehards throwing in the towel in the face of an especially dreadful Japanese monster epic, and Jon finally headed up to the room, where he grabbed a couple hours of restless sleep.

Only now was the shock beginning to subside.

Only now was he able to begin exploring the significance of what had happened last night. Last night, afterwards, he had tried to squeeze what had happened out of his mind, filling his head instead with the harmless, distracting images of old movies. Now, the next morning, Saturday, he sat by the window at the airport, watching the ground crew scurry around a Boeing 727, sipping his flat Coke and replaying the events of the night before on the movie screen of his mind. Jon remembered waking up after being struck by Billy Comfort with a pole of some kind, and remembered looking up at Billy and realizing that the pole was the handle of a pitchfork, a pitchfork Billy was a second away from jamming into Jon. He knew he should roll out of the way, but Billy's foot was pressed down on his chest, holding him there, firm, for the pitchfork's downstroke. . . .

And then a shot, and another, and Jon had seen two thin streams of blood squirt from Billy's chest, and Billy was knocked off his feet, allowing Jon to roll clear, which he did, the pitchfork sinking into the earth next to him. For a moment, both Jon and the pitchfork trembled. Meanwhile, Billy had flopped on his back and died.

Jon got to his knees, turned, and saw Nolan. They looked at each other, a look that had a lot in it.

Then Jon saw Sam Comfort, whom Nolan had evidently knocked down but not out, rearing his head above the high weeds that had hidden him from Jon's vision, and Sam Comfort had a great big goddamn gun in his arms, a *shotgun*, and was lifting its twin barrels to fire them into Nolan, and Jon yelled, "Nolan! The old man!"

And instinctively Jon clawed for the .38, yanked the gun from its holster, and wrapped both hands around the stock and aimed and squeezed the trigger. Just as Nolan taught him.

The shot was an explosion that tore the night open.

And Sam Comfort.

Old Sam caught it in the chest, high in the chest, about where one of the bullets had struck his son, and fell over on his back, much as his son had.

Jon got to his feet, but didn't go over to where Sam was. Nolan was already leaning down to examine the man.

Jon said, "Is he? . . ."

"Not yet," Nolan said.

"What should we do?"

"We should get the hell out of here."

"And . . . leave him ... to bleed to death?"

"Yes."

"Jesus, Nolan."

"Listen, what is it you think we're doing here? Playing tag-you're-fucking-It? We've robbed these people, Jon, and killed them. Now what do you think we should do?"

"Get the hell out of here," Jon said.

So now, having spent a shocked, pretty much sleepless night, Jon tried to begin facing up to the fact that he'd—damn it!—that he'd killed a man. Every time he admitted that to himself, every time the phrase *killed a man* ran through his mind, his stomach began to quiver, like that pitchfork in the ground.

Sure, the prospect had always been there, ever since he first teamed up with Nolan, on that bank job. And yes, there'd been blood before; people around them had died, violently—his uncle Planner for one. Bloody brush fires like that could spring up around a man like Nolan at just about any time. But reacting to such brush fires was one thing, and starting them something else again. Nolan had introduced Jon to a world of potential violence, but together they, had never initiated violence. Never before, anyway. This time—pitchfork or no pitchfork, shotgun or no shotgun—this time, Jon and Nolan had invaded someone else's home territory, had initiated violence, and people had died. This they had known, these thoughts Jon and Nolan had shared in that look they exchanged after Billy's death; a loss of innocence for Jon, for their relationship, that they could recognize even through the smoke and nylon masks.

That the Comforts were perhaps bad people, evil people, was weak justification at best, rationalization of the most half-assed sort, and made Jon wonder just how he and Nolan were any different from Sam and Billy Comfort.

It all came down to this: Jon had killed a man.

And it made him sick to think it.

"Sorry I took so long," Nolan said, sitting down across from Jon at the window table. He took a bite of his sandwich, a hamburger identical to Jon's. "Damn thing's cold. Was I gone *that* long?"

"It was cold when they brought it."

"Goddamn airports. I told you we should've just grabbed a hot dog at one of those stand-up lunch counters."

"I hate those things, Nolan. Standing at those lousy little tables, getting your elbow in somebody's relish . . ."

"Yeah, but the food's hot, isn't it? And not so goddamn expensive."

Jon had to smile at Nolan's consistently penny-pinching attitude. Here they'd picked up, what? Over $200,000 from the Comforts' strongbox last night, and the man is worried about nickels and dimes. Jon could figure why Nolan had taken so long in the can, too: he'd waited till the non-pay toilet was vacant.

Nolan noticed Jon's smile, weak as it was, and said, "You feeling better, kid?"

"I'm feeling all right."

They really hadn't talked about it yet, but it was there.

"You can't let this get you down."

"Nolan, I'm all right. Really."

"I believe you."

They were silent for a while, each nibbling at his cold, lousy hamburger as if it were a penance.

Jon glanced around to make sure a waitress wasn't handy to overhear, then said, "Are you sure the money's going to be okay?"

"Sure."

"What about the . . ." Jon gestured, meaning the two guns, which along with the money were in one of Nolan's suitcases.

"Don't worry," Nolan said. "The baggage goes through unopened, I told you."

"Don't they have an X-ray thing they can run the baggage through?"

"That's just for carry-on luggage. Shut up. Eat."

Neither one of them finished their hamburgers. Nolan left no tip. When Nolan wasn't looking, Jon left fifty cents. After all, the waitress wasn't necessarily to blame for the hamburgers being cold.

Fifteen minutes later, boarding passes in hand, they were standing in line while a pair of female security guards, armed, took all carry-on luggage, right down to the ladies' hand bags, and passed it through the massive X-ray scanner. Ahead of them in line a few paces was a college-age kid with curly brown hair, similar to Jon's, wearing jeans and a green corduroy shirt tucked in over a premature paunch, carrying a Radio Shack sack.

"Hey, Nolan," Jon whispered.

"What."

"That kid up there."

The kid was presently handing the Radio Shack sack to the security guards and being checked through with no trouble.

"What about him?"

"Isn't that a wig he's wearing? Take a look. That isn't his hair, is it?"

"Maybe not," Nolan admitted. "So what?"

"Well, it just seems strange to me, a young guy like that, wearing a wig."

Nolan shrugged.

So Jon shrugged it off, too; maybe the kid was prematurely bald or something. Like the paunch. Weird, though—young guy with no fat on him elsewhere, no hint of a double-chin, and here he has a gut on him.

Jon stepped up and smiled at the two security guards, both of whom were pretty and blonde, and allowed his brown briefcase to be slid into the X-ray. Then he and Nolan stepped through the doorlike framework that was the metal detector. On the other side Jon picked up his briefcase of comics, wondering offhand if X-rays had a negative effect on pulp paper.

They climbed the covered umbilical ramp to the plane, boarded, and were met by the flight attendant Nolan had met at the hotel. She was a knockout brunette who, for some reason, looked vaguely familiar to Jon. She gave him a brief, similar where-have-I-seen-you-before look, and then she and Nolan traded longer looks of a different sort, Nolan saying, "Morning, Hazel."

"Good morning, Mr. Ryan," she said, and she and Nolan made eyes for a second. It was damn near embarrassing.

They passed through the forward, first-class compartment and past the central galley, where the fourth and final flight attendant (a dishwater blonde not quite as attractive as the others) was already fussing with filling plastic cups with ice. They continued on into the tourist cabin, where they took the very last seats in the rear of the plane, near the tail. Only a few people were on board as yet, but Jon and Nolan had been toward the front of the metal-detector line, and the plane was going to be close to capacity.

Jon was having problems with the briefcase: it was so jammed full of comics and stuff, he hadn't been able to get it shut again, since the security guard checked it. He was struggling with it in his seat, and it got away from him and flopped out into the aisle, in the path of another passenger.

It was the kid in the wig, still lugging his Radio Shack sack.

The contents of Jon's case were scattered in the aisle, and Jon and the guy in the wig bent over and began picking the books up.

"I've got some of these," the guy said, holding up a Buck Rogers Big Little Book. He had a soft voice, or at least was speaking in a soft voice. He seemed almost shy.

"Really? You a collector, too?"

"No. I read them as a kid."

"You don't look that old."

"They were my older brother's."

"Oh. Well, thanks for the help."

"Hope I didn't damage them or anything."

"Never mind. My stupid fault."

The guy in the wig smiled a little—a very little—and went on toward the rest rooms in back of Jon and Nolan's seat. He stepped inside the first one.

"Must be nervous," Jon said. "Plane isn't even off the ground and he's going to the can already."

Nolan hadn't been paying much attention. "Maybe it's his first flight," he said.

12

NOLAN LOOKED OUT the double-paned window as the Detroit airport flowed by, the plane beginning to make its move down the taxiway. Above him, the little air vent was blowing its stale, recycled air down into his face and, as he looked up to turn it away from him, he noticed the FASTEN SEATBELTS and NO SMOKING signs flash on in red letters, and he buckled up. About that time, Hazel's voice came over the tinny intercom and reminded anyone who hadn't yet complied with those two requests that now was the time.

He didn't really like planes that much, didn't care for flying. He didn't feel in control on a plane and preferred traveling by car, where he himself could be behind the wheel. Years ago, he had traveled by train fairly often, but train service in this country had gone to hell, and buses were a pain in the ass and slower than walking. So he was adjusting, finally, to the jet age, despite his firm belief that if God had wanted men to fly, he'd have given them parachutes.

They had the three-abreast seat to themselves, though the unused third was presently being taken up by the briefcase of comic book crap that Jon had lugged aboard. Right now, the cabin pressure was making its abrupt increase, and Jon was making faces, swallowing as he popped his ears. Nolan did the same, with less facial contortion.

Hazel's voice came on the intercom again, while two of the other flight attendants stood, one at the front of the tourist compartment and the other halfway down the aisle, going through the oxygen-mask-and-emergency-exit ballet to the accompaniment of Hazel's narration. When that was over, one of the flight attendants came walking down, checking to see if all smokes were out and seat belts fastened, and when she came to Jon and Nolan, she asked Jon to please put his briefcase under the seat in front of him. Jon explained that it wouldn't fit under there, and she took it away from him, paying no heed to his protests, and put it in a closet compartment opposite the rest rooms that were right behind them.

For a while, Jon sat there, looking like a kid whose favorite toy got taken away. Then he said, "Nolan."

"What."

"Get a load of that."

The kid who'd collided with Jon's briefcase of comic books a few minutes before, the same kid Jon had noticed was wearing a wig, had come out of the john from behind them and was now heading back up the aisle.

"Get a load of what, Jon?"

"That kid in the green shirt."

"What about him?"

"That isn't his stomach."

"What?"

"He's got something under his shirt."

"No kidding."

"No, really, Nolan, something bugs me about that guy. Why's he playing dress-up? Wearing that wig. Carrying something under his shirt."

"Maybe it's old comic books."

"You can laugh if you want to, but that's a weird kid,

take it from me . . . and don't say 'takes one to know one.'"

"Would I say that?"

"You'd think it."

"You got me there."

The plane had stopped now, having reached the end of the taxiway, and out the window Nolan watched a DC-8 land, bouncing twice on its motionless tires, making blue smoke as rubber met concrete, and then settling down. The soft throb of the 727 jets began to build as the plane started to move, picking up speed fast, shoving Nolan and Jon back in their seats. The nose of the plane lifted, and they headed for the gray sky, Detroit slipping away rapidly under them.

The seat belt and no-smoking sign soon winked off, and Nolan loosened his seat belt but left it buckled. The captain's voice came out of the intercom and went into the standard flying-at-assigned-altitude-and-estimated-time-of-arrival spiel. According to the captain, the overcast day would be turning into rain here and there up ahead, but he anticipated smooth flying nevertheless. Sure.

On the whole Nolan was pleased with the way things had worked out at the Comforts. Maybe *pleased* wasn't the word—more like *satisfied*. The take had been over two hundred thousand (he hadn't counted it, except for a fast shuffle through the strongbox of cash), and they'd got out with their asses intact, in spite of the foul-up. What more could he ask?

It was, of course, unfortunate that Jon had had to shoot a man; but something like that was bound to happen sooner or later, and the kid had been exposed to the rough side of the business before, so it wasn't like he'd been a complete virgin. Last night, what had happened had left Jon silent and shocked, but today he was as talkative as ever, and seemed only slightly depressed. And sleepy. Nolan would bet his share of the take that the kid hadn't slept more than a couple hours, at most.

If he had his way, it wouldn't have happened. He'd sure as shit tried to plan around any overt violence. But what the hell, you can't shelter a kid forever; if you do, he's going to suffocate. He figured Jon would get over it. There'd be a scar, but Jon would get over it.

Yes, the kid would have a rocky conscience for a while, Nolan knew, but that was the way it should be. It wasn't healthy to feel good about killing a man, even a man the likes of Sam Comfort. When killing gets easy, a man is less than human, in Nolan's opinion, and a man who likes killing isn't a man at all. Besides, it's bad for business. Society and its law-enforcement agencies take a much dimmer view of killers than they do of thieves, possibly because most of society fits into that latter category, to one degree or another.

Anyway, it was over and done, and they were sitting pretty: pretty rich, and pretty lucky to be alive, and pretty sure nothing could fuck up at this late date. Nolan did feel a little bad about holding onto the two guns. Normally, he'd have got rid of them immediately, since they'd been fired on a job—especially when they'd been fired and killed somebody on a job—which these guns had. And he would get rid of them when he got back, after he had seen to it Jon and the two hundred thousand were returned safely to that antique shop in Iowa City. He would've asked Bernie for a fresh gun when he returned the Ford early that morning, but Bernie wasn't there yet, so he'd decided to risk holding onto the .38s for a short while. But it was not good policy to do so, and it grated on him even now, thinking of those two guns down in the suitcase in the hold, nestled next to all that cash. Even Jon, over their mid-morning brunch (two bucks for a goddamn stinking *cold* hamburger!) had expressed concern about the guns, which had pleased him because it showed that Jon was getting more perceptive about things that counted, and irritated him because the kid had spotted a flaw in Nolan's supposed perfection.

Hazel was coming down the aisle, looking very nice in the tailored flight attendant outfit, with its soft, light colors. She stood beside their seat, leaned down, and asked, "Can I get you gentlemen something to drink?"

"I thought you were working first class," Nolan said.

"I was, but since you were riding tourist, I traded off with one of the other girls."

"Can you do that?"

"If you're senior flight attendant, you can."

"Oh, you got rank, huh?"

"It's called age. But it was kind of silly for me to do."

"How's that?"

"Well, this junket's such a short hop, I'm not going to have much of a chance to do anything besides serve a few drinks and pick up the empty cups."

"Yeah, but anything, just so you can be close to me, right?"

Hazel said to Jon, "I see why you need all three seats. One for you, one for him, and one for his ego."

Jon said, "He's just talking big so nobody notices he's airsick. If he had his way, we'd be traveling by covered wagon."

Hazel laughed, and Nolan did too, a little. Nolan ordered a Scotch and Jon a Coke, and let Hazel go.

"She's a nice lady," Jon said.

"Yeah. She lives in Chicago. One of those high-rises on the lake. Has lots of days off, she says. Maybe I'll be able to get in and see her now and then."

"Chicago isn't much of a drive from the Tropical, is it?"

"An hour, if the traffic is bad. Only, I hope I won't be at the Tropical much longer."

"With half of last night's take in your sock, you shouldn't have to be."

Nolan nodded, then said, "Say, kid."

"What?"

"I, uh, never really, you know, thanked you for last night."

"Thanked me?"

"Yes, goddammit. You did save my fucking ass, you know."

"Well, you saved mine. So what?"

"Yeah. So what."

They both sat back and tried to look gruff. Nolan was better at it than Jon.

"Hey, Nolan."

"What"

"That kid. The one with the wig."

"I don't want to hear about it."

"He's headed up toward the front going up through the first-class compartment."

Nolan had no comment.

"I don't know, Nolan, something weird about him, I tell you. Something's going on with that kid."

"Aw, shut up. Go to sleep for half an hour, or go get one of your funny-books and read it or something."

They sat in silence. Five minutes went by, and then the dull little bell sounded that signaled the intercom coming on.

The captain again.

"We'll be having a little change in course this morning, ladies and gentlemen. We'll be rerouting our plane directly to the Quad City Airport at Moline. Those of you who were headed there anyway shouldn't mind this little detour as much as the others."

The captain's lame attempt at humor had the reverse of its intended effect: it was easy to see past his superficially light, joking tone and tell something was wrong, very wrong, and the murmur of passenger concern swept through the plane like a flash flood.

He continued, "Now, I don't want anyone to panic. Everything is in control." The captain hesitated. "But I feel you should be aware that we have a man with a bomb aboard . . . and he's just chartered himself a plane."

13

LIKE ALL FLIGHT attendants, Hazel knew she might one day be involved in a skyjacking, but she wasn't overwhelmed with fear by the prospect. At one time she would have been: at one time she'd been deathly afraid of flying itself.

Fifteen years ago, when she'd first applied for a job with the airlines, she'd requested ground duty. Then, when she got into the program, she'd begun a gradual change of mind, even after that grueling week of intensive training under emergency conditions, in which she'd had to overcome some of her fears, anyway, just to live through the damn thing. The advantages a flight attendant had over girls on the ground were many, with fewer hours of work for the same amount of pay perhaps the biggest lure of all, and oh, those gorgeous travel possibilities! Factors like that had whittled away at her flying fears, and the statistics had helped, too. Knowing that a plane was safer than a car, for instance, if for no other reason than that the man behind the controls was a professional, not a sloppy amateur like most motorists. That if an engine went out, there were three more to take its place. That practically every little town in the world had some sort of air strip, so a landing spot was always close at hand.

Of course, there were accidents, and air accidents have few—if any—survivors. A flight attendant friend of hers (not a close friend, but more than an acquaintance) had been on a plane that was struck by lightning and went crashing to the ground, providing a fiery death for the friend and fifty-some other people aboard. Don't think Hazel didn't have a sleepless night or two over that.

But every profession had its risks, and for a woman, being a flight attendant was pleasant, even glamorous, no matter what Women's Lib had to say about it. In fact, liberation of the sexes had only gone to show what a good job the flight attendant had: males had begun clamoring for the jobs, and many a tired businessman had recently had the disappointment of looking forward to a bouncy blonde stewardess and getting instead a brawny blonde steward.

Skyjacking was one risk, however, Hazel hadn't had to consider fifteen years ago; during the first years of her career the term hadn't even been coined. The hijacking of a commercial airliner was so infrequent that the industry, from board of directors down to flight attendants, thought of it as some bizarre, freak occurrence, an incomprehensible and frightening crime, but certainly no large-scale threat to air travel itself. The 1968 rash of hijackings—twenty-one in all—changed that attitude quickly enough, and skyjacking became a major worry in the minds of all airlines personnel. Hazel included.

She'd seen the public's reaction turn from amusement

and titillation to terror and rage. Early on, the skyjackings (usually to Cuba) seemed a free vacation of sorts; even *Time* magazine urged skyjacked passengers to "enjoy the experience," and "make the most of your side trip by doing a little shopping," telling them of the "magnificent" Cuban beach, and noting that "the food is excellent, too." Was it any wonder she'd overheard a passenger wistfully wishing for a skyjacking experience to brighten the boredom of a business trip? She'd winced as one federal aviation official had gone so far as to announce that skyjacking "sure takes the blahs out of air travel."

And then violence had changed the amusement to terror: a pilot shot in the stomach by a skyjacker angry because the ransom money delivered to him was short of what he'd asked; a black militant beating crew members about the head with a revolver, threatening passengers with similar abuse; a prisoner being transported by plane finding a discarded razor in the john and, holding that razor to a flight attendant's throat, demanding his own Cuban "side trip"; and, of course, the chaotic violence of the Arab-Israeli airline war, the world witnessing the destruction of a $23 million aircraft, a Pan Am 747 melted to junk by exploding dynamite charges.

With a feeling of disappointment verging on despair, Hazel and other flight attendants had watched as the FAA tried desperately to find means of fighting skyjacking, most of those means proving ineffective at best, ludicrous at worst. A bulletproof shield protecting the pilot was one FAA official's suggestion, as well as barring the cockpit door. Just how this would dissuade a skyjacker, who'd have plenty of unprotected hostages aboard to choose from, was not explained, unless Hazel and her sisters were to wear bulletproof bras and issue bulletproof shields to each passenger. The FAA then distributed to ticket-sales personnel a "psychological profile" of the "typical" skyjacker, but skyjackers seemed able to get past ticket counters without hassle despite the "profile," which was general to the point of silliness, anyway, the most solid "fact" being that "the average skyjacker is a man between sixteen and thirty- five years of age." The FAA's next move was to create a system of armed guards for planes, in response to a request heard repeatedly from the public, and the Sky Marshal Program was the result. This particular concept terrified Hazel from the start: the idea of a shoot-out at 30,000 feet was enough to terrify anybody. The "unwritten directive" of the sky marshal was well-known among flight attendants: "If a skyjacker uses a flight attendant as a hostage, shoot the flight attendant to reach the skyjacker." Swell. In actual practice, however, the sky marshals were little threat to either skyjackers or flight attendants. Typical of their ineffectiveness was the successful skyjacking of a jumbo jet to Cuba, though three sky marshals were present on the plane, as well as an FBI agent. The Sky Marshal Program was discontinued some time ago, but the recent rash of skyjackings by Cuban refugees and other social outcasts had prompted the FAA to reinstate it. This Hazel saw as more of a gesture than an anti-skyjack measure.

The only way to effectively deal with a skyjacker was to stop him before he got on a plane. She remembered when the first real step was taken: the search of carry-on luggage before passengers boarded the plane. Suddenly guns and knives were commonly found dumped in waste cans in airport johns. Then metal detectors came into use, and X-ray of carry-on luggage, and skyjacking again became an exception, not a rule. Still, skyjackings had been pulled off by men using "guns" that turned out to be plastic ball-point pens and combs; one skyjacker proclaimed himself a human bomb, while his "explosives" turned out to be rolls of candy mints stripped to his body. The most hair-raising of the boomerang effects caused by the use of metal detectors was the switch skyjackers had made to nonmetallic devices such as homemade bombs. Hazel shuddered at the thought of that. Though neither situation exactly appealed to her, she would much prefer facing a man with a gun than a man with some unstable, patchwork homemade explosive device.

And now she was doing just that.

A young man of perhaps twenty years of age was aboard with what appeared to be a pocket calculator in his hand — claiming he was prepared to blow up the plane if his demands were not met.

JoAnne, the youngest of the other three attendants on board, had come to Hazel with a look of stark panic in her eyes. Hazel was in the galley section, which was between the first-class and tourist cabins, getting drinks ready. JoAnne said, "He says he wants to talk to the head stewardess. That's you, Hazel."

"Who says what?"

"A kid. He says he's got a bomb. He wants to talk to you."

"All right. Now, JoAnne. Listen to me. Keep your head on. Are you all right?"

"Yes."

"Where is he? Up forward?"

"Yes."

"Okay. Are you all right, JoAnne?"

"Yes."

"Okay. You stay right here. Don't say a word to

anybody. I see him up there. Green corduroy shirt and jeans? With a beer belly?"

"Yes."

"Okay, then. You stay here. You might finish getting these drinks ready for me."

"Yes."

He was just a boy, really. A kid. With damn freckles, yet. He was wearing mirror-type sunglasses, which she didn't believe he'd been wearing when he came aboard, and he was wearing a wig. Why hadn't she noticed that wig before? Damn.

"Are you the head stewardess?"

"I'm the senior flight attendant, yes."

"Hazel?" he said, reading her name off the badge on her breast pocket. "Your name is Hazel?"

"Yes, it is."

"Hazel, I have just now pressed some buttons that have armed a bomb that is on this plane, in my suitcase in the cargo hold of the plane. If my fingers touch this—" he indicated the black plastic calculator— "just so, the bomb will explode and all of us won't be here anymore."

"Do you want to see the captain?"

"Yes. You tell him to come out here."

She entered the cockpit the greenish glow of the instrument panel brighter than the overcast sky out the forward windows.

Captain McIntire, a handsome gray-templed man in his early forties, a married man with two kids, and a confirmed letch who'd tried a hundred times to get in Hazel's pants (unsuccessfully), turned in the left-hand seat and grinned wolfishly, saying, "How's tricks, Hazel?"

Beside him, the copilot, Willis, suppressed a groan. He was a thin guy with a pockmarked complexion and short brown hair, in his late thirties. He hated McIntire, and it showed sometimes. Behind McIntire was the navigator, Reed, a balding, fleshy, middle-aged man with no discernible personality, as far as Hazel knew—an invisible man as gray as that sky out there.

Hazel did not play it cute. No, Captain, tricks are not good, she thought, and said, "We have a skyjacker aboard. He's just outside the cockpit here."

The three men traded expressions of disgust that masked fear.

McIntire cleared his throat, but his first words came out a squeak, anyway. "Send him in, damn it."

"He wants you to come see him."

Reed said, "Whoever heard of hijacking a plane out of Detroit?"

Willis said, "We did. Now."

The captain turned over the controls to his co-pilot and rose from his seat. He wasn't grinning anymore.

Hazel stood next to the captain while the boy told him about the bomb. He spoke in a voice that was soft and seemingly calm but had a faint tremor in it. Then he made his demands. He said, "Two hundred thousand dollars in cash. This is how I want it: ten thousand twenty-dollar bills. Radio ahead and have the cash delivered to the Quad City Airport at Mo-line. We will, naturally, fly directly to the Quad City Airport. Then we'll fly somewhere else."

The captain stood there for a moment, waiting.

Then the boy said, "That's all I want. Go back and fly your plane. Tell your passengers the situation."

Which the captain did.

The skyjacker asked Hazel, "I believe you're working in the tourist-class section, aren't you?"

"Yes, I am."

"My seat is in tourist. I'll walk back with you."

So now she was serving drinks, the skyjacker sitting among the chattering, fidgeting passengers like just another victim, giving no indication to anyone he was the villain of the piece.

But when she served Nolan his Scotch, he said, whispering, "It's the kid in the wig, isn't it?"

Surprised, Hazel nodded.

"What's the airline's policy in a skyjacking?"

"Do what the man says, what else?"

"How does the kid claim he'll detonate his bomb?"

"He's got a pocket calculator wired to do it, he says."

Nolan thought a moment, then said, "I think he's bluffing. I don't think he has any bomb on board."

"We have to assume otherwise," Hazel said.

"You do," Nolan said. "But I don't."

And a chill ran up her spine. For a moment, for reasons she didn't wholly understand, she was afraid of her last-afternoon-and-night's bed partner. For a moment this man calling himself Nolan—though he was flying under the name Ryan, for "business purposes," he'd told her last night—frightened her far worse than the young skyjacker sitting a few feet away.

14

BY THE TIME the plane landed at the Quad City Airport, most of the passengers were smashed. Common practice during a skyjacking was for flight attendants to serve free drinks to anyone who wanted one, and that included just about everybody on board; the exceptions were sitting in front of Jon and Nolan: a trio of nuns, who looked like they could use a good, stiff drink, at that.

The booze had had its intended calming effect on the passengers, creating an atmosphere not nearly as tense as it might have been. Other factors had also helped lessen the tension, the main one being that the skyjacker had remained anonymous to his fellow travelers, and had not gone about waving a gun and shouting obscenities and generally reminding everybody they were sitting on a flying powder keg. Of course, the tension was there, underneath it all, and if the atmosphere was strangely like a party, it was a less than jolly affair—a going-away party, perhaps, or a bankrupt company's last Christmas fling.

Even Jon had fallen prey to the free-flowing liquor; he wasn't much for hard booze, but the role of skyjacking victim was upsetting enough to his nerves for him to gladly switch from Coke to Bourbon and Coke and its soothing, analgesic powers. Jon had downed only two of them so far, but he was feeling the glow. He and Nolan hadn't spoken much since the news of the plane's enforced change of destination, and now he glanced at Nolan and regarded his older friend's expressionless, tightjawed demeanor. He figured Nolan's stern countenance meant one of the following: either Nolan was pissed off, or was putting together a scheme of some sort, or both.

Anyway, Jon thought, something was wrong. Nolan hadn't had anything to drink since that first Scotch, which he'd barely finished. That wasn't like Nolan, turning down free drinks. Turning down free anything.

For some reason, Nolan was taking this skyjack thing very, very hard, and it puzzled Jon.

"Hey," Jon said, whispering. "This'll work out all right. What's the harm? I mean, it got us home quicker, didn't it?"

Nolan said nothing.

"I agree with you," Jon continued, "about the kid in the

wig. I don't think he put a bomb on board, either. Or anyway, if he did, I don't think he's the type to set it off."

Nolan was shaking his head now. He looked disappointed.

"Nolan, what's wrong?"

They were speaking low anyway, because of the holy trio in the seat ahead, but now they lowered their voices to less than whispers, reading each other's lips, really, a communication just this side of telepathy.

"Don't you get it?" Nolan said. "Don't you see it yet?"

"Get what? See what?"

"We're screwed."

"Huh?"

"Your pal in the wig, Jon. He's screwed us. Shoved it in and broke it off."

"What d'you mean? How are we worse off than anybody else on the plane?"

Nolan took Jon's almost-empty glass of Bourbon and Coke away from him, set it on the floor, said, "You better stick to straight Coke in the future, kid. You aren't thinking too clear."

"I don't . . ."

"Okay, Jon. We're on a skyjacked plane. Now, what's the best we can hope for? What's the best thing that can happen in this particular situation?"

"Well, I suppose the best thing that could happen would be for somebody to take that supposedly rewired calculator away from the skyjacker. That would put the plane back in the hands of the good guys, right?"

"Okay. Then what."

"Everybody rides off into the sunset, I guess. Except for the skyjacker. He goes straight to jail, do not pass Go, do not collect two hundred thousand dollars. Right?"

"Half right. The skyjacker isn't the only one who goes straight to jail and doesn't collect two hundred thousand dollars."

"What?" The clouds began to lift inside Jon's head. "Oh. Oh Jesus."

"Yeah. Oh Jesus. Even if they could grab this guy before he's done any damage, the 'good guys,' as you call them, would still have to assume there's a bomb on the plane. Which means the bomb squad'll be called in and . . ."

"They'll fluoroscope all the luggage. Shit. Oh shit. And all our money? All our beautiful money? . . ."

"We'll just have to forget it. Best we can hope for is to leave the airport fast as possible, before people start asking embarrassing questions. Hope to Christ they don't trace the luggage to us. My phony name'll lead them nowhere, that's one good thing. You're using your right name, but your luggage has nothing suspicious in it. I just hope nobody remembers we were traveling together. I hope Hazel'll cover for us—a little, anyway. I hope a hell of a lot of things, frankly."

"Jesus, Nolan. We can't just let all that money go. . . ."

"We have to. I been trying to figure a way to save it, but I can't find one. That money isn't the only thing in that damn suitcase, don't forget."

"I haven't forgotten, Nolan. I wish I could, but I haven't."

The guns, Jon thought, the goddamn guns.

The two .38s they'd used at the Comforts'. The two .38s they'd used to *kill* the Comforts. Bad enough to have to try and explain two hundred grand in cash, but two hundred grand in cash and two revolvers, both of which might be traceable to a multiple killing and robbery . . .

Jon didn't want to think about it.

"And," Nolan was saying, "that's what happens in the

best of all possible worlds. The other possibilities are even more depressing. Such as, maybe there is a bomb on board, and the skyjacker gets rattled, and we all get blown to hell, in which case we won't sweat the money. Or, the guy lets some of us off the plane and keeps some hostages, and then gets rattled, and our money gets blown up. Or the goddamn skyjacking is a success, and the guy gets away, and the bomb squad moves in to work on the plane and . . . well, it goes on like that. No matter how you figure it, Jon . . ."

"We're screwed."

Hazel was coming down the aisle. She stopped beside them and said, "Now that we've landed, he's having me ask among the passengers for volunteers to be hostages. He's going to keep ten people on the plane and let the rest go."

"Then what?" Nolan said.

"He says he'll let the hostages go when the ransom's delivered. When we take off again, just the pilot and copilot and navigator and yours truly'll be aboard. And the skyjacker, of course."

"Has he made any more demands?"

"He wants two parachutes."

"Why two?" Jon asked.

Nolan grinned. "Because he's smart. He learned that trick from the best skyjacker of 'em all, of D. B. Cooper. Asking for more than one insures him that the chutes won't be sabotaged."

"Why?" Hazel wanted to know.

"Because with two parachutes, he might make somebody else jump along with him."

Hazel still didn't understand. "Certainly not the pilot or copilot or navigator," she said.

Nolan nodded. "Certainly not."

Hazel swallowed. "Let's hope the powers that be don't consider us flight attendants expendable."

"Any other demands?"

"Just that we aren't to reveal his identity to the other passengers. As you said, he's smart. He figures the fewer people that get a good, long look at him, the better. This way, he'll just blend into the crowd."

Jon said, "I don't know, he looks pretty obvious to me, with the wig and sunglasses and everything."

"Not really," Nolan said. "Most of the passengers on this plane are businessmen. They just figure him for some hippie kid or something; a fairly likely suspect, maybe, but not much more so than anybody else."

"D. B. Cooper," Hazel said, "was dressed like a businessman. Suit and tie, topcoat oxfords. Like most of the people around you."

Nolan asked, "Has he told you where you'll be flying yet?"

"No. Mexico, though, don't you suppose? Parachute out into some flat area, where somebody'll be waiting to pick him up?"

"Maybe."

"I'm supposed to be asking for volunteers right now. But I'm not asking you. I don't want you. Understand? We'll have plenty of volunteer hostages, and I don't want you two to be part of them. Especially you, Nolan or Ryan or whoever you are. I get the feeling you're the hero type, and I don't want you grandstand-playing me into getting blown to pieces."

"I'm telling you, Hazel," Nolan said, "that kid doesn't have any damn bomb on board. Take it from me, I'm a judge of character if there ever was one. That kid just doesn't have the balls for it."

They'd been keeping their voices down anyway, but she leaned over and whispered, so as not to take any chance of ruffling the feathers of the nearby nuns, and said, "It doesn't take balls to blow up a plane, dummy. Just a little dynamite." And she headed back up the aisle, skirt flashing over those fine, long legs of hers.

"So what are we going to do, Nolan?"

"I'm glad Hazel gave us an out. A hostage is one thing we don't want to be. We can't afford to stay. Or you can't, anyway. Now, soon as you get off this plane, you get your ass back to Iowa City, got me?"

"You got an idea, Nolan?"

"I might have."

"What is it?"

"You just let me do the thinking, and do as I say."

"Yeah, I know, I know, mine is not to reason why. You're the mastermind and I'm the flunky."

"Think of yourself as second in command, if it softens the blow."

Thirty seconds later, the captain's voice came over the intercom: He instructed all the passengers, except those who had volunteered to stay on board, to come forward and disembark. Everyone but the hostages began to rise from their seats, the businessmen straightening their ties, grabbing their briefcases; women fussing with their hair, tidying themselves in preparation for the photographers who'd be waiting out there; even the three nuns were smoothing out their habits. Everyone but the hostages, and the skyjacker of course, began to move forward.

Except Nolan.

Who slipped into the nearest of the two johns around the corner from their seat and, giving Jon a look that said, "Keep quiet and do as I told you," sealed himself inside the cubicle.

And now Jon stood alone, at the rear of the aisle, everyone else trailing on up toward the front, excluding the handful staying behind; Jon began up the aisle, hesitantly, wondering what the hell to do.

He could almost identify with the skyjacker; they were about the same age, after all, and had both got in over their heads in daring, potentially violent endeavors in pursuit of riches. And Nolan stowing away like this meant one thing to Jon: the skyjacker was in for it. Nolan was going to do God-knows-what to that poor kid, and Jon didn't know who to be more worried for, Nolan or that dumb-ass skyjacker.

And then a realization hit Jon, a short, hard jab that almost knocked him down: Nolan was wrong!

Nolan's assumption that the skyjacker had not planted a bomb on the plane was clearly false. Otherwise, why would the skyjacker take the trouble to let the bulk of the passengers disembark here at the Quad Cities? The kid evidently had a conscience of sorts, and didn't want to blow any more people to smithereens than he absolutely had to! The stupid fucking hypocrite.

Jon didn't know what to do. Should he warn Nolan? Go back and tell him, explain the logic of it, pull him out of that damn can and fuck the money, just get the hell out of here? What good was Nolan going to do jumping the kid, anyway? *Nolan!* he screamed in his brain. *There* is *a bomb on this goddamn plane!*

But it was too late to go back. He was passing beside the seat where the young skyjacker was sitting calmly, just another brave volunteer hostage, as far as anyone could tell. A sudden rush of indignation ran through Jon. He wanted to grab that little shit by the shoulders and shake him till his wig fell off. What kind of fucking monster could do a thing like this? Didn't the bastard have any respect for human life at all? How could the son of a bitch coldly plant a bomb on a plane and treat life and death like some casual goddamn thing?

Jon glared at the skyjacker as he passed him, but in the reflecting mirror-sunglasses, he saw only himself.

15

HE LOOKED OUT at the airport. It was a modest affair, two creamy-brown brick buildings joining a central tower, some hangars off to the side. You could set this airport down in the lobby at O'Hare and no one would notice. Its relative smallness was one reason he'd picked it. He'd chosen Detroit as takeoff point and the Quad Cities as ransom drop, partially because neither airport had been involved in a skyjacking before; the Quad City Airport was especially poorly equipped for such a contingency. He realized the money would probably have to be flown in from Chicago, but that was just a twenty-minute flight, and since he'd had the pilot call the demand ahead, the money could almost beat them there. Here at the Quad Cities, a skyjacking would be more than the local enforcement agencies could handle, and the people flown in on the spur of the moment from Chicago would be disoriented and, in teaming with local people, disorganized; by the time anyone was at all prepared to deal with him, he would be gone. But had he chosen O'Hare, for example, he'd have had to face a damn anti-skyjack task force.

He was more than aware of the harsh fate dealt out to others who'd engaged in this particular crime: there were so many instances of FBI snipers dropping skyjackers, he couldn't keep them all straight in his mind, though one recent episode was vividly clear to him: a skyjacker had been cut in half, literally, by the close-range blast of an FBI agent's shotgun. Consideration of such facts had led him to the choice of a relatively "small-town" airport, but even then, he knew that overconfidence was insanity. For that reason, he had sent the stewardess out to pick up the money. He was not about to stick his head outside the plane and get it blown off his shoulders by an FBI marksman.

He watched as the attractive brunette flight attendant walked out on the runway, per his instructions (the transfer of money was to be made in full sight of the plane, in broad daylight), while a heavyset, sour-faced probable FBI man in a brown suit, carrying an attaché case and two parachutes, walked out from the airport complex and met her. He handed her the case of money so reluctantly, you'd have thought it was his, then gave her the chutes and headed back. She returned to the plane. No apparent attempt at trickery.

He smiled, sat back in the seat.

The flight attendant, Hazel, brought him the attaché case.

"Sit across the aisle," he told her, "and open the case."

"You want *me* to open it?"

"Yes. I'm sorry, but it might be sabotaged. I might snap it open and release a gas or something. I have to be careful, you can understand that"

"Of course," she said.

She sat across from him, opened the case.

There was no gas, no explosion.

There was, however, a lot of money. Rows and rows, stacks and stacks, of green packets, packets of cash still in their Chicago bank wrappers.

"Shall I count it?" she said.

"Please. There should be ten thousand twenty-dollar bills."

It took a while.

"All there," she said.

"Thank you. Close the case, please."

She did, and handed it to him. He laid it on the seat beside him, next to the tape recorder.

She looked at him strangely. She was a very pretty woman; striking eyes, the color of her name. She looked something like Carol, as a matter of fact, only brunette instead of blonde. She said, in a surprisingly kind voice, "What's a nice kid like you doing in a situation like this?"

When he'd researched other skyjackings, he'd found that his goal was different from most. Funny, too, because his would *seem* the most likely goal. But it wasn't. Many skyjackers did it for glory; he wanted none of that. True, the adventure of it had been appealing to him, but the publicity meant nothing. He had no desire to become a folk hero, à la Rafael Minichiello or D. B. Cooper; and he certainly didn't want to see his name in the papers! Some skyjacked out of death wish, suicidal tendency; if he had any of that, he didn't know it. Much skyjacking was political protest and/or the seeking of political asylum, the skyjackings to Cuba being the most obvious example of that. But there was no political motivation to his skyjacking, although a disillusionment with the American Dream had had something to do with his transition from straight, conservative citizen to air pirate. But who was not a pirate, after all, when the Establishment reeked corruption, from the White House on down? And he'd seen how the great capitalist system worked, hadn't he? The protestant work ethic he'd obeyed so religiously, only to be swindled and squeezed and screwed out of his savings and his youth and his ideals by those good capitalists at Dream-Land Realtors. Still, he was no protester; he cared nothing for politics. His was an admittedly selfish goal he shared with few skyjackers; D. B. Cooper and a handful of others, that was all.

So, when the stewardess asked him for his reason, he was almost anxious to clarify himself.

"I need the money," he said.

And she smiled—couldn't help herself—and nodded, almost sympathetically. "I know what you mean," she said.

He wanted to tell her that he didn't want to hurt her, but he knew it would sound silly, hypocritical to the point of absurdity. But he really didn't. And he didn't want to hurt himself, either, but if they forced him to, he knew he'd have to consign this plane and the pretty stewardess and himself and all his hopes and dreams to a fiery hell. The only consolation was, it would be over in an instant. Like turning off a TV. Press the button, and boom. No pain.

He told her, Hazel, to let the hostages off the plane, and she made the announcement over the intercom, as the hostages were scattered all about the plane, having remained in their own seats, at his request. He'd felt it best not to let them huddle together, as people in such situations often do; that type of thing could lead to an uprising or some other sort of half-assed heroism, which he could do without.

He was glad to see the hostages go. Relieved. He'd felt the same earlier, when he watched the other passengers leave. It was as if a great weight on him was gradually being lessened. Now, with just the crew and the single stewardess left aboard, he felt almost at ease. The pilot, copilot, and navigator—and the stewardess, too, for that matter, much as he liked her—were the equivalent of military personnel who had taken on a risk-prone job and were prepared, to some degree, anyway, to die in the line of duty. His conscience was taxed far less by their presence than by that of the passengers. Having the passengers around him had proved much more disturbing than he'd expected. The possibility of pressing some buttons on that specially wired calculator and destroying the plane and people on it had been just that: a possibility, a hopefully unlikely eventuality that Those-in-Authority might force him to, if they were foolish. The responsibility would not be his. But once on the plane, with faces all around him, lives all around him, his emotionless, laboratory theorizing blew up in his face like a misjudged experiment; his rationalizations strained at the seams, as the faceless ciphers of his game plan turned out to be flesh-and-blood human beings, people, not pawns. And this hand had trembled around the plastic case of the calculator.

Now, though, the passengers were gone, the last remainder of them trickling out at the stewardess' guidance, and the hand around the calculator no longer trembled—even if its palm Was a trifle sweaty.

With the hostages safely off the plane, the stewardess came to him for further instructions. He told her to inform the captain to take off immediately.

And they did. The stewardess remained in the cockpit, and he strapped himself into his seat while the plane taxied down the runway and lifted its nose in the air. Once the plane had leveled out again, he unbuckled and, taking along only the calculator, left his seat and went forward and knocked on the cockpit door.

The stewardess answered, and he told her to tell the captain to come out and talk to him.

He didn't want to go in there, in the cockpit. He didn't

want to be contained in that small area with those three probably very capable men. And he wanted to show them, the captain especially, that he, the skyjacker, was in command now; when he told the captain to come, the captain damn well better come.

The captain came.

And said, "What's our destination?"

"I think we'll be going to Mexico," he said.

"We'll need fuel for that."

"I know. You can refuel at St. Louis."

The captain nodded.

"I would like all of you," he said, and he nodded toward the stewardess, "to remain in the cockpit throughout the rest of the flight. Understood?"

They indicated they understood.

"Captain, I want you to fly this plane at low altitude and low speed, from here on out."

"How low?"

"Five thousand to six thousand feet, speed one hundred and twenty-five nauts. Fly a straight course to St. Louis. I know the terrain. I'll know where we are. No stunt flying, please."

"You intend to jump?" the captain asked. "I thought you said Mexico. . . ."

"Maybe. That's my concern. I think you can understand that it's to my benefit to keep you, as well as the people you'll be in constant contact with on the radio, in doubt as to exactly what my intentions are. By the way, you'll notice very soon that the rear ramp exit is down. I'll be lowering that ramp as soon as you return to the cockpit."

The captain got a knowing look in his eye; what he knew was this: the ramp was ideal for use by a parachutist. Only 727s and DC-9s had such ramps.

"Do not assume, captain, that I'm going to jump immediately. Maybe I will. Maybe I won't. But I am aware that a warning light on your panel lights up when the ramp is lowered, so I am lowering the ramp now, so that you will not be able to pinpoint when or if I've jumped. If I haven't knocked on the door by the time we approach St. Louis, you'll know I'm gone."

"Which airport in St. Louis?"

"It doesn't matter. The FBI will be at whatever place I pick. Tell you what. Feel free to select the one you like best. You're the captain, after all."

The captain's eyes tightened, while the stewardess seemed almost to enjoy the put-down, and when the captain returned to the cockpit, she remained in the doorway to say something to the skyjacker. What she said was, "It's a little late to be saying this, but try not to do anything you'll regret."

He smiled. "It is a little late for that."

"Well. Enjoy your money, anyway."

"Thank you. I'll do my best."

She disappeared into the cockpit.

He went back to his seat and waited while the pilot brought the plane to a lower altitude; then he walked to the rear of the plane to let down the ramp. Seats the flight attendants used during takeoff were folded against the door, and above that was the handle, which he pushed all the way to the left, pulling the door in; just outside the door, on the left, was the stair release control, a little box with a lever in it, which he pushed outward. The ramp lowered. There was an immediate suction effect, which he'd anticipated, and he braced himself accordingly. The wind noise and jet roar were deafening, but there was no pressurization problem at this altitude. Ears aching, face whipped by gusting air flow, he smiled out at the ramp, the little mini-flight of stairs that would allow him to jump from the plane with ease.

He went back to his seat, where the attaché case of cash waited. He took off the wig, the sunglasses. He stripped off the green corduroy shirt; beneath it he wore a thin black cotton pullover, long-sleeved, and the single emergency chute, strapped to his stomach. He wasn't about to use the two chutes he'd asked for. He knew they would be bugged; they would be hastily but well armed with homing devices that could lead the FBI and everybody right to him. He would wait a while, and, one at a time, throw those chutes out, to send the posse on a wild goose chase or two.

He settled back in the seat and, breathing easily for the first time in hours, began to relax. The project was going well. Flawlessly. Admittedly, it had been harder to execute than to plan—well, not harder, really, but more taxing emotionally. It was one thing to coolly plot, to engage in deliberated planning, to rehearse his lines in his head, and quite another thing to carry out all of that in a plane filled not with Xs on a diagram, but human beings.

And that was the element he couldn't plan for, the human element, and it had worried him, both at home and on the plane. Blueprints were fine for building houses; diagrams were great for putting together electrical systems. But human beings weren't as dependable as diodes, and he realized something could go haywire, despite his thorough engineering; he knew some human could throw a wrench in the works.

In fact, he had thought he'd spotted someone who might be just the person who would throw that wrench. Sitting next to that kid, that curly-haired guy with the Big Little Books and comics, was a rock-faced man with dark hair and mustache and narrow eyes that had an almost Oriental cast to them; he'd felt those eyes on him, boring into him, and had noticed the stewardess, Hazel, talking to the guy more than was perhaps natural. He'd almost decided the guy was a FBI man or sky marshal or something, but to his relief the guy hadn't stayed around as a hostage, which would have been a good indication that he was a law enforcement agent of some kind who'd happened to be on the flight. He hadn't banked on having someone like that aboard, and was glad to find his suspicions were groundless.

Some time passed, and he went back to the noisy aperture and tossed out the first of the parachutes.

He went back to his seat, the calculator still in hand but not so firmly now, and he sat and watched the land go by. He'd told the pilot to fly a straight course, not wanting to be overly specific about precisely what course he wanted (since that would alert everyone that he indeed did intend to jump soon) but knowing that if the pilot wasn't pulling something, Highway 67 should be in constant sight. It was. It was important for Highway 67 to be within reasonable walking distance when he jumped, in order for Carol to pick him up as planned. He checked his watch; time was working out okay. All was running smooth, then.

A few minutes passed, and he went back to the ramp and threw out the second parachute.

He sat down again, looked out the doubled-paned window. Missouri was rolling by. Some of it was hilly, but most was relatively flat farmland, which was what he was after. Soon he should spot the landmark he was looking for and make his jump. He prepared himself, checked out the chute; got the C. B. out of the Radio Shack sack, which had been under the seat in front of him; he set it on his lap, atop the attaché case. He still had the calculator in hand,

and hadn't decided whether to take it along or not; probably wasn't wise to leave anything behind he didn't have to, but maybe there was some freak chance of the thing detonating the bomb on the plane, with the impact of his fall.

He watched out the window, the familiar landscape gliding by. And then he saw the landmark—and red barn whose slanting roof bore white letters advertising MIRACLE CAVERNS—and he got up. He clipped the C.B. onto his belt, tucked the attaché case under his arm.

Now was the time.

He walked down the aisle, toward the ramp at the rear of the plane; the opening beckoned him, a gateway to freedom, to a new start for Carol and him. And as he walked by the rest rooms, a hand reached out and clamped onto him by the wrist, shook the calculator from his hand. Then a fist crashed into his jaw, damn near breaking it, knocking him back on his butt.

His mind reeled: *someone sneaked on the plane at Moline,* he thought, *damned FBI sneaked someone aboard!*

Then he looked up and saw who it was.

That hard-faced S. O. B. with the mustache.

Who was now on the floor, in the aisle, scrambling after the calculator, which had flipped between some seats. The guy had a look of pain on that scowling face of his, from the mingled wind-noise and jet-screech coming from the open ramp door, a harsh, grating sound that was working on the guy's eardrums.

The skyjacker was used to the sound, as the ramp door had been open some time now; but the guy with the mustache had been hidden away in the rest room, apparently, where the sound had been muffled. Which meant the guy was somewhat incapacitated, but the skyjacker was still hesitant about retaliation: the guy was big, and looked mean as hell, and was probably armed.

He knew he was close enough to that door to make a successful jump, no problem; he had the money. Why not go for it?

But the guy with the mustache had seen him, sans wig, sans sunglasses, sans any disguise; and would be able to report exactly where he'd jumped. Which meant one thing: the skyjacker would be caught.

He'd never considered the possibility of capture, really; he'd always thought it was either/or, heaven or hell—a bundle of money and make a new life, or no life at all. Now, with capture, he'd have prison to face; life imprisonment, perhaps, and the same for Carol. . . .

In the three seconds it had taken the skyjacker to make these realizations, the guy with the mustache had retrieved the calculator from between the seats, though he was still on his hands and knees. He looked up with an expression of annoyance; he was a mean-looking S. O. B., all right, like an Indian with a grudge.

The skyjacker swung his attaché case and caught the guy on the chin, throwing him back, on his back, apparently unconscious. The skyjacker went to retrieve the calculator from the man's hand—best not leave that behind. . . .

But the guy reached out a big hand and grabbed him by the ankle, and yanked, and he fell on his ass in the aisle, hard, and the attaché case of money went skittering out of his hands, landing a few feet away from the open ramp door. With that suction effect, the case would get pulled outside in a second if he didn't reach it first, and on his hands and knees he crawled after it, like a grossly oversize infant. He got his hands on the case, the suction of the open door tugging at the skin on his face, the wind slapping him, and he felt something come down hard on his back.

A foot.

And then the guy said something; he had to yell, scream it really, to get his voice above the jet roar and wind. He said, "If I let you up, will you behave?"

Now it was the skyjacker's turn to yell. "Yes!"

"I shouldn't," the guy said, still screaming, "I should kick your goddamn ass out of this plane."

But the pressure subsided; the foot went away.

He got to his feet and looked at the guy. He had expected the guy to be fuming, but he still seemed more annoyed than enraged. And another surprise: he had no gun, at least not in sight.

And that gave the skyjacker a burst of courage.

He knew he was close enough to that door to make a successful jump, no problem. He had the attaché case in his hands. Why turn the money over to this guy when there wasn't even a gun pointed at him? Why give up now, after working so hard and coming so close?

He lurched forward, shoved a hand into the guy's chest, pushing into him, knocking him off balance.

But it wasn't enough.

The guy with the mustache lashed out with a fist as big as a softball, and the skyjacker tumbled back, head spinning, knocking against the edge of the open ramp door; then the suction got hold of him and he was gone, unconscious or damn near but somehow instinctively clutching the attaché case to him, falling down those steps into the gray sky.

Four

16

SOMEONE DROPPED something in the kitchen and woke Jon.

He sat up in bed, startled by the sound, and found the room around him dark, which startled him too. When he lay down late this afternoon, it was still light outside—or as light as an overcast day can be—but now it was pitch black. He'd fallen asleep and now, as he checked his watch, he found he'd slept well into the night.

Damn, he thought. He'd only meant to rest for a moment, just lie down and relax a while, really. Not fall asleep. He hadn't even had a chance to call Karen yet, to tell her he was back in Iowa City. Too late for that now. Damn. How could he fall asleep, with Nolan literally up in the air like that? What the hell was wrong with him?

Another sound.

Someone was moving around out in the kitchen.

Breen, Jon thought. Just Breen, up having a post-midnight snack.

They had left Breen at the antique shop while they went to Detroit for the Comfort heist; Breen hadn't felt like traveling right away, with his wound and all, and besides, his car windshield was shot out, so they'd left him to mind the store.

When Jon got back late this afternoon, Breen had been full of questions.

And complaints.

"You might've called," Breen had said, "and let me know how the goddamn thing came out. I had a stake in it, too, you know."

And Jon had said, "Well, you know Nolan. He couldn't see wasting a long-distance call when we were coming right back, anyway."

Breen had mumbled something about what a cheap-ass Nolan was, and then went on to ask, well, what the hell happened at the Comforts, anyway? What Jon told him sounded like a good news/bad news joke. First the good news: they had successfully stolen over $200,000—even the part about the Comforts dying was good news to Breen, who was glad to see them go. Then came the bad news: the skyjacking.

And Breen had started to moan and groan—such a terrible thing, losing all that money. Jon was in no mood to listen to him bitch, and went upstairs and fixed himself a ham and cheese sandwich. Breen came up and ate half of Jon's sandwich and asked Jon if he could recommend some place to get a new windshield put in his car. Jon told him where he could get that done, then went into his uncle Planner's bedroom and lay down for a short rest.

So now it was the middle of the night and he was awake, finally, and someone was moving around out there, in the kitchen. Probably Breen, but Jon wasn't sure; he was nervous, not having heard from Nolan yet, and he wondered if it could be an intruder of some sort out there. He pulled open the nightstand drawer by the bed and got out one of his uncle's .32 automatics.

He stalked through the pine paneled living room and slowly edged toward the archway that led into the kitchen. The lights were on in there, bright and white. Breen, probably; but he kept the .32 leveled out in front of him, just the same.

He lunged through the archway and into the kitchen, and Nolan was sitting at the kitchen table, eating some breakfast cereal.

"Don't shoot, kid," Nolan said, holding up his hands, one of them with a spoon in it, dripping milk down on the table.

"Nolan!"

"Quiet," he said. He put down his hands. "You want to wake up Breen? He's down sleeping like a baby in your bed, and I don't want that talkative son of a bitch waking up and making me explain things all night."

"Nolan," Jon said, incredulous. He sat down at the table with him, set the .32 next to the box of breakfast cereal. "Where'd you come from?"

"Caught a bus at St. Louis. Where's the god-damn sugar? These fucking Grape Nuts are supposed to be naturally sweet, but they taste like wood shavings to me. Get me the damn sugar."

Jon got him the sugar, rejoined him at the table.

"Well, Jesus, Nolan."

"Jesus what?"

"What happened? What happened?"

"I caught a bus at St. Louis, I told you." He ate some cereal and grinned at Jon as he chewed.

"Oh, for Christ's sake, Nolan, quit being so goddamn cute. I can't stand it. Tell me what happened!"

"Say, have you been listening to the news, kid?"

"No, I fell asleep, damn it."

"I'd like to know what they're saying on the news. I'd like to know what they're saying about our money, which ought to've been found by now. Turn on that radio on the counter. The news'll be on in five minutes."

"I'll turn it on in five minutes. How'd you get in here, Nolan? The doors were locked and you don't have a key."

"I don't need a key to get in a house. So you were sleeping, huh, kid? Your concern for me's overwhelming."

"Yeah, well, Nolan, I'm sorry I fell asleep, but could you please tell me what happened?"

"Not much to tell. I stayed in the can. Nobody caught on I was in there, least of all the skyjacker. I waited till all the hostages were off the plane, waited for that stupid kid to make his move to jump, and then I took that calculator away from him. Didn't want him blowing me up, whether by accident or not, and that wasn't unlikely with him jumping with a damn detonator in his hand. So I took it away."

"Then you decided he *did* have a bomb on the plane?"

"Yes," Nolan said, and he ran through the same chain of logic, proving the bomb's existence, as had Jon. Which would have given Jon a certain sense of satisfaction, if he hadn't been so confused about so much else.

"But I don't get it, Nolan. Why'd you even bother staying on the plane? Certainly not just to take the calculator away from the guy, to save the airlines their plane. You're not the knight-in-white-armor type."

"I had my reasons." And he grinned again, chomping cereal. "I got a surprise for you, kid."

"Surprise? What do you mean, surprise?"

"Well, just before the plane got to St. Louis, I knocked on the cockpit door and told Hazel and the pilot and everybody what I'd done. That I'd taken that thing away from the skyjacker, before he jumped. And I was a hero. They were so grateful they could shit. When we landed and were getting off the plane, I asked Hazel if she would go get that briefcase of funny-books out of that closet across from the john, because if I left that behind, my young nephew—that's you—would never forgive me. She obliged, and before the FBI or anybody could ask me a thing, the hero of the hour, briefcase tucked under his arm, excused himself to go to the can and instead went out and caught a cab and went straight to the bus station. After all the time I'd spent boxed up in that crapper in the plane, you'd think it would occur to those jokers I'd already had ample opportunity to relieve myself. But it didn't."

"Now let me get this straight," Jon said, not understanding at all. "You mean you went to the trouble of asking for that briefcase, just to be nice to me? That doesn't sound like you, Nolan. No offense, but you're not the most thoughtful man I ever met. I mean, it's a nice surprise, but . . ."

"That's not the surprise," Nolan said. He reached down and brought the briefcase up from the floor beside him; he put it on the table.

"Hey," Jon said, "that's not my briefcase."

"No, it isn't."

"It looks something like it, but that's not it"

"Open it. Go ahead."

Jon snapped the case open.

"Jesus," he said.

The case was full of money.

Crammed with packets of money; packets of $20 bills, in bank wrappers. Thousands and thousands of green dollars.

"The skyjacker's money," Jon said. Awe struck. "You switched on him!"

"Yeah," Nolan said. "Easy as pie. He went forward to boss the pilot around, and I just sneaked out of the can, switched his briefcase with yours, and sneaked back again."

"Damn, you switched on him! You switched on him. Nolan, you're a genius. And an even trade, at that. We hardly lost a cent on the deal."

"I wouldn't say that, kid. Every serial number on every bill in that briefcase was recorded by the feds before they let it go, you can bet on it. We'll have to peddle it to a fence, at a loss."

"But we'll still come out okay, won't we?"

"We'll come out okay."

"What about *our* money? The money in your suitcase? Who gets that?"

"I'm not really sure. It's confiscated, of course, so I suppose the government ends up with it. Don't they always?"

"Nolan . . . how in hell could you know the money would come in a briefcase so similar to mine?"

"I didn't. That was dumb luck. The way I had it figured was I'd have to switch the contents of the two briefcases, and that would've been tougher. But possible. Maybe I would've had to tangle with the skyjacker sooner that way, and that could've been risky."

"What happened to the skyjacker, then? Did he make his jump or what?"

"Well, we had a little scuffle. I hit him pretty hard and he fell out of the plane. His chute opened, late, but it opened. I told the pilot later that the kid waited till we were almost to St. Louis before jumping, which I said to throw them off, since it's to our benefit if he gets away, with everybody assuming he has the money. I suppose he's alive."

"I kind of hope so."

"Yeah, me too, but only because it helps us if he is. Otherwise, after what he put us through, he could break his goddamn neck and be okay with me."

"He's just another kind of thief, Nolan. Like you. And me."

"No. There's a difference. He's an amateur. I . . . we . . . are professionals."

Jon smiled. "I don't think I'm much of a pro, but thanks anyway, Nolan. There's only one thing I regret. . . ."

"What's that? You still brooding about killing old Sam Comfort? Don't. You couldn't have shot a more deserving soul."

"Oh, not that. That does bother me, don't think it doesn't. But that wasn't what I meant."

"What did you mean?"

Jon leaned forward and spread his hands. "Well, it's great you got the money, and I don't want you to take this wrong, but if you'd have just told me what you had in mind, I could've emptied the briefcase and taken my comic books with me. Do you have any idea what those things are worth? How hard they are to find? Do you know that . . ."

Nolan put some more sugar on his cereal

Epilogue: Crash-landing

17

CAROL FOUND HIM in the high grass off to the side of the highway, behind a billboard advertising a bank savings plan. She was relieved she'd had so little trouble finding him; he'd told her, over the C.B., that he'd overshot their target area just a little, but that he could still make it to Highway 67, and when he had, he'd told her of the billboard and she'd found it—and him—with ease.

He was a mess. He was as pale as a cadaver, the black pullover and jeans streaked with the mud from the farmer's field he'd landed in, and probably from stumbling and falling in the miles of other fields he'd trudged through to get to the highway. His discomfort was obvious: he was curled up in a crumpled ball, like a wad of paper littered along the road; he was clinging to the brown attaché case like a drowning man clutching something buoyant.

Still, he was in one piece, and it could have been worse. She'd expected it to be worse. If he'd been bloody and twisted, she wouldn't have been surprised; she knew his jump had been a bad one, that he'd hit hard and wrong, even if he hadn't said so, because even over the C.B., the pain was evident in his voice, no matter how he tried not to show it.

"Baby," she said, "how bad is it?"

"Not so bad," he said. "Collar bone's broken, I think."

"Oh baby . . ."

"It can wait till we get home."

"Can't we? . . ."

"No. We can go to the hospital at Canker, soon as we get back. We'll say I fell down the stairs or something. Here. Take the money back to the car. Do that first, then come help me. It'll look less suspicious. Okay?"

"Okay."

She returned to the car and opened the trunk. Cars were whizzing by, but no one was paying any attention to her. She put the attaché case in and started to close the trunk lid, then stopped. She was curious. She wanted to see what $200,000 looked like. She wanted to see what they'd gone through hell for. So she snapped open the case, for a quick peek. . . .

Bright four-color covers in plastic wrappers flashed up at her: pirates in outer space, ray guns, and rocket ships.

She shut it again, quickly, as if maybe she hadn't really seen what she'd seen.

She didn't know why, or how, but the elaborate plan, the "project," had gone wrong. Dreadfully, disastrously, absurdly wrong. A practical joke turned back on the joker.

And, like all good jokes, it was funny, or would be: in their old age, perhaps, they could reflect on this foolish episode and its ironic result with some amusement. Yes, she thought, Ken and I might laugh about this someday.

But not right away.

Not today.

She closed the trunk, wondering what to do. It was obvious Ken didn't know anything had gone wrong; that he still thought he'd got off the plane with an attaché case full of money. And now was certainly not the time to tell him any different.

Now was a time to go back and put her arm around her husband's waist and help him to the car and get him to a hospital. Later would be a time for mending wounds, for putting pieces back together.

She got Ken settled in the back seat, and he was asleep almost at once.

Now was a time for going home. Alive and free, and going home, Carol thought. That in itself was a lot, wasn't it?

She got behind the wheel.

About the Author

Max Allan Collins, who created the graphic novel on which the Oscar-winning film *Road to Perdition* was based, has been writing hard-boiled mysteries since his college days in the Writers Workshop at the University of Iowa. Besides the books about Nolan, the criminal who just wants his piece of the American dream, and killer-for-hire Quarry, he has written a popular series of historical mysteries featuring Nate Heller and many, many other novels. At last count, Collins's books and short stories have been nominated for fifteen Shamus awards by the Private Eye Writers of America, winning for two Heller novels, *True Detective* and *Stolen Away*. He lives in Muscatine, Iowa with his wife, Barbara Collins, with whom he has collaborated on several novels and numerous short stories. The photo above shows Max in 1971, when he was first writing about Nolan and Quarry.

Hard-boiled heists by *Max Allan Collins*

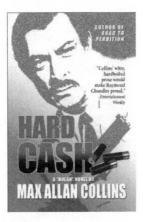

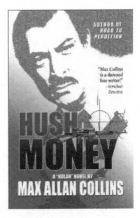

FLY PAPER
Max Allan Collins
162 pages $13.95
ISBN: 978-1-935797-22-7
"Collins is a master."
Publishers Weekly

HARD CASH
Max Allan Collins
150 pages $13.95
ISBN: 978-1-935797-23-4
"Witty, hardboiled prose."
Entertainment Weekly

HUSH MONEY
Max Allan Collins
180 pages $13.95
ISBN: 978-1-935797-24-1
"A damned fine writer!"
Armchair Detective

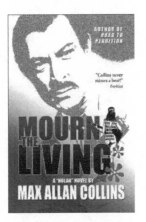

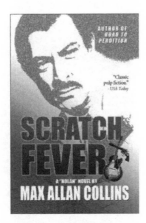

MOURN THE LIVING
Max Allan Collins
172 pages $13.95
ISBN: 978-1-935797-25-8
"Never misses a beat!"
Booklist

SCRATCH FEVER
Max Allan Collins
164 pages $13.95
ISBN: 978-1-935797-26-5
"Classic pulp fiction."
USA Today

SPREE
Max Allan Collins
212 pages $14.95
ISBN: 978-1-935797-27-2
"An exceptional storyteller!"
San Diego Union

Killer for hire: 5 classics by Max Allan Collins

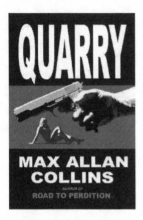

QUARRY
Max Allan Collins
234 pages $14.95
ISBN: 978-1-935797-01-2
"Packed with sexuality."
USA Today

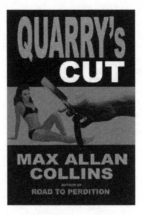

QUARRY'S CUT
Max Allan Collins
182 pages $13.95
ISBN: 978-1-935797-04-3
"Classic pulp fiction."
USA Today

QUARRY'S DEAL
Max Allan Collins
190 pages $13.95
ISBN: 978-1-935797-03-6
"Violent and volatile."
USA Today

QUARRY'S LIST
Max Allan Collins
164 pages $13.95
ISBN: 978-1-935797-02-9
"Never misses a beat!"
Booklist

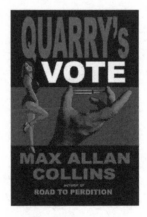

QUARRY'S VOTE
Max Allan Collins
214 pages $14.95
ISBN: 978-1-935797-05-0
*Quarry versus a
political cult.*

*Nobody's
harder-boiled
than Quarry.*

*Each title with
a new Afterword
by the Author.*

> "If [it] moved any faster you'd have to nail it down to read it." **Elmore Leonard**

New York private eye Miles Jacoby

EYE IN THE RING
Robert J. Randisi
July 2012 $12.95
ISBN: 978-1-935797-40-1
"He's one of the best."
Michael Connelly

BEATEN TO A PULP
Robert J. Randisi
July 2012 $12.95
ISBN: 978-1-935797-41-8
"A masterful writer."
James W. Hall

HARD LOOK
Robert J. Randisi
July 2012 $12.95
ISBN: 978-1-935797-42-5
"Stripped for speed."
Loren D. Estleman

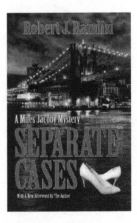

FULL CONTACT
Robert J. Randisi
July 2012 $12.95
ISBN: 978-1-935797-43-3
"Shades of James M. Cain."
Harlan Ellison

STAND-UP
Robert J. Randisi
July 2012 $12.95
ISBN: 978-1-935797-44-9
"Last of the pulp writers."
Booklist

SEPARATE CASES
Robert J. Randisi
July 2012 $12.95
ISBN: 978-1-935797-45-6
"Best of the Jacoby books."
Jeremiah Healy

Short story collections from *Perfect Crime Books*

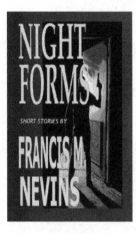

NIGHT FORMS
Francis M. Nevins
378 pages $16.95
ISBN: 978-1-935797-00-5
"Tricky, stark, brutal."
 Publishers Weekly

NOIR 13
Ed Gorman
250 pages $14.95
ISBN: 978-0-9825157-5-4
"Strong collection."
 Publishers Weekly

THE HOLLYWOOD OP
Terence Faherty
246 pages $14.95
ISBN: 978-1-935797-08-1
"Writes this era like he was there." Crime Spree

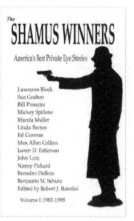

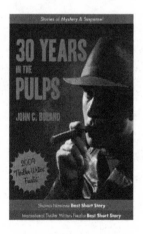

THE SHAMUS WINNERS
Volumes I & II
$14.95 each
Vol I ISBN: 978-0-9825157-4-7
Vol II ISBN: 978-0-9825157-6-1
"Must-have items."
James Reasoner

THE GUILT EDGE
Robert J. Randisi
232 pages $13.95
ISBN: 978-0-9825157-3-0
"One of the best."
 Michael Connelly

30 YEARS IN THE PULPS
John C. Boland
346 pages $14.95
ISBN: 978-0-9825157-2-3
"Style, substance, versatility." EQMM

Private eyes at large

MURDER UNSCRIPTED
Clive Rosengren
122 pages $8.00
ISBN: 978-1-935797-19-7
"Straight from the 1940s. Luscious."
Booklist

CROSS ROAD BLUES
Troy D. Smith
198 pages $13.95
ISBN: 978-1-935797-09-8
"Drugs, murder, a little Voodoo, the blues."
Bill Crider

BLUE BAYOU
Dick Lochte
252 pages $12.95
ISBN: 978-1-935797-33-3
"Darkly comedic New Orleans—food, music, bullets." Kirkus

THE PINK TARANTULA
Tim Wohlforth
174 pages $12.95
ISBN: 978-1-935797-11-1
"Tough as they come. Well worth your time."
Mystery Scene

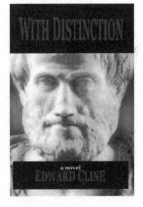

WITH DISTINCTION
Edward Cline
152 pages $14.95
ISBN: 978-1-935797-21-0
"Hanrahan is a great character!" Booklist
"Fine series." Jas Reasoner

LAST ISLAND SOUTH
John C. Boland
244 pages $12.95
ISBN: 978-0-9825157-8-5
"Superior thriller." Publishers Weekly on *Hominid*. Murder in Key West.

2012 Shamus Nominee
Private Eye Writers of America
Best Paperback

*The President's dirty little secret
is worth your life.*

*Hayes Rutherford did his stint in Vietnam, flying a rescue
chopper that earned him the nickname "Last Chance."
And he was a standup guy forty years later when someone
had to take the fall for a Pentagon billing scandal.*

*After 18 months in a federal pen, Hayes figures he's done
with the Washington crowd. Working for his daughter
at a Hollywood P.I. firm, his biggest challenge is
keeping the talent sober.*

*But when rumors ping the White House that somebody
is shopping an ugly movie script about the war-hero President,
Hayes looks like suspect number one. He's about to have his show
cancelled for good, because there are some stories that political
spin doctors can't fix.*

LONG PIG   James L. Ross   320 PAGES $15.95 ISBN: 978-1-935797-10-4

By the author of *Death in Budapest*
"Twists straight out of John le Carre." *Publishers Weekly*

Made in the USA
Middletown, DE
20 July 2015